I0626594

The 25th
Napata's Dream

R L Scott

LBP

First printing, first edition

ISBN: 978-1-7363861-4-9

PUBLISHED BY LION'S BROOD PUBLISHING, LLC

Printed in the United States of America

Prologue

Piye rode his stallion each morning to assess himself and the steed. Without fail, they negotiated the final hurdle. Each morning, the pharaoh envisioned a good day.

Chapter One

The sand lizard scurried into the dune, anticipating the hell that approached. Heavy horse hooves trampled the desert floor on the west side of Lake Nasser. The sound of gallops and feint screams coming just beyond the dune filled the pitch-black night sky. The air was crisp and dry, absent of the wet pleasure of humidity and wind. Only the moonlight allowed for any observation or directional insight. Chenzira made it to the top of the mound as a single arrow zipped past his face, nearly decapitating the young man.

Whether through loss of balance or with purpose, Chenzira tumbled down the decline. His long braids flapped around his almond-shaped head. As he rolled downward uncontrollably, the sand covered his wiry, mocha-hued fame and white tunic made of sheep's wool. With each impact from the fall, Chenzira released a grunt, almost a whimper. Once he reached the bottom of the sandbank, he turned over to rest on his back. His chest heaved up and down, searching for air to fill his lungs. His body ached, not from the fall so much. His legs became unstable, and his arms succumbed to a pulsating soreness from days of fleeing to survive, to live. The source of the screams appeared atop the bank. Mothers with children in tow and elderly men in their robes navigated the unsteady sand as they shouted Kushite proverbs in prayer to their gods. Perhaps they numbered twenty or thirty. The gods were not listening that night. Arrows found their mark, penetrating adults and children alike. Crimson blood splattered amid the cold and dusty landscape. They fell in unison, some lifeless before they hit the ground. The others cried out in agony, searching for lost limbs and their innards while falling down the embankment. Blood soaked the sand red, creating a violet hue under the revealing moonlight.

The *Musims*, also known as the Believers, reached the apex of the sand dune. They remained there on horseback, large bows in hand, numbering fifty in their collective. As the horses neighed with impatience and the moonlight glimmered off their bronze-scaled chest plates covering their black, Egyptian-cotton tunics covered in bronze pieces and Blue Crow *kepresh* helmets, the male and female warriors appeared battle-hardened with just a touch of arrogance. They quickly dismounted and reloaded their bows with arrows from their quivers. And without mercy, the musims released another volley into the wounded and downtrodden Kushite villagers. The arrows found their mark once more, penetrating skulls, limbs, and midsections. The screams soon died down. Only the sounds of alligator-bone arrowheads separating flesh from muscle remained. The shafts went through and through. There was no sight of Chenzira.

Gahiji's Egyptian horse-drawn, two-wheeled war chariot, or *mrkbt*, arrived behind his warriors. He stood on the golden, light semicircular vehicle with reins in hand. Gahiji was the leader of the musims and the only pursuer with an armored chariot. He stopped the chariot with a single tug of the horse's harness and removed his helmet, revealing a long, cobra tattoo on his right cheek. The stallion's nostrils flared with abrupt disapproval. Gahiji leaped from the chariot quickly and held tightly to the hilt of his *khopesh* sword, a fine sickle-sword from his family's legacy.

"Find the boy," Gahiji shouted.

5

Gahiji was a hunter, a personal guard for the pharaoh. He was unsure of the day of his birth, but he estimated he was thirty turns around Re, his "god of light." He was a true Egyptian with a bronze-like complexion. He was tall for such a crafty warrior, standing nearly six-foot tall. Gahiji wore his hair in a single braid, revealing the scar on his cheek from a past battle. He squinted as he espied his surroundings, searching into the dark landscape for Chenzira. The stoic stare on his face had never changed. Gahiji was a calculating fellow, yet his facial features never changed with each emotion. He contemplated. He stared. While the other musims searched the bodies for the boy, his gaze found one musim, a muscular warrior of Kushite decent. He sauntered over to the young man who breathed heavily with excitement and waved him over.

"Yes, Chief?" the warrior said nervously.

Gahiji grabbed the warrior by the shoulder gently, ensuring an amiable engagement. "Fine shooting, young warrior," Gahiji said with a big smile.

"Thank you, Chief," the warrior responded. A smile slowly appeared on his childish expression. "The Seth bastards were fast but not fast enough."

Gahiji chuckled playfully. He shook the young man in a congratulatory fashion. "Yes, indeed. They are known for their quickness." While smiling, Gahiji continued, "However, one of your arrows nearly hit the boy. Let us remember, one day he will lead us. Until then, no harm is to come to him." Gahiji continued his playful shake.

The young warrior's smile dissipated slightly. His eyes remained locked with Gahiji's. "Yes, of course, Chief. It will not happen again. I let the excitement of the chase get the best of me."

"It is okay. I understand the thrill of the hunt, but we are not hunting boar," Gahiji said as he ceased shaking the warrior. "Go and search with the others."

As the young musim walked away, Gahiji's gaze followed his every step. There was something cold and unforgiving in his stares, certain resentment with a well-hidden snarl. Before his focus suffocated the steely warrior, Gahiji took a deep breath and tasted the cool, bitter breeze. He stared at the many tattoos that covered his body, each representing a fallen foe. It was considered an honor to carry the image and spirit of your enemies, and he did not disappoint. He took a knee and let his rugged fingers sift through the grainy earth at his feet.

Gahiji had been trailing Chenzira for nearly a fortnight and questioned the orders he received from Piye. Why am I here? He had served the pharaoh from the beginning, before the Nubians gained complete control of Egypt. He was there at the battle against Tefnakht. Gahiji remembered the carnage, the blood, and the glory that went to the Kushites. If only his wife and daughters were there to witness his retribution for the past. The memories resurfaced relentlessly to near madness. He was a long way from Memphis.

Out of the darkness, his lieutenant approached from behind. "Chief Commander, the boy has seemed to disappear. Perhaps, he made his way to Aswan."

Gahiji stood and brushed the sand from his knee. "Yes, he's quite crafty. Make camp and post guards there and there. He cannot be far. Finish the Seth-loving scum."

"Sir, I doubt he's anywhere near here. Should we not continue north?" The lieutenant said in a monotone voice.

Gahiji stared at the man with the sharpness of a thousand daggers. He then raised one eyebrow and tilted his helmet-less head slightly. "That is a beautiful longbow." He pointed to the hand-carved, wooden weapon that the lieutenant held in his grasp.

The lieutenant stared at the bow and smiled as one would to an anecdote that escaped him. "Thank you, sir. I made it myself from the finest acacia. It is flexible yet sturdy enough for the arrow to penetrate most forms of armor."

"Is that so? You mind?" Gahiji said as he motioned to the lieutenant to hand him the longbow.

The lieutenant graciously handed Gahiji the weapon with two hands. His nerves began to ease, and his smile grew larger, exposing the century's lack of proper dentistry. "It is a fine weapon, sir."

Gahiji accepted the composite bow and gazed at its slender, wooden frame. He held the weapon in a simulated launching fashion, extending the bowstring slowly. He aimed to the sky and released the string, creating a sharp, thumping sound. "Impressive," Gahiji shouted. "Very strong." He faced the lieutenant and reached out a single hand. "Might I have an arrow?"

The lieutenant pulled a single arrow from his quiver and handed it to Gahiji, nervously and graciously. "Perhaps, the chief commander would like a game of hunting after this assignment?"

Gahiji placed the arrow in the bowstring, effortlessly. Initially, he aimed to the night sky. He caught a glimpse of Orion and Sirius floating in the heavens. Gahiji believed that Osiris looked down on the warrior from his kingdom, *Duat*. Taking on more glances at the stars, Gahiji lowered his aim and released the sharp projectile. As if through destiny and purpose, the arrow found its target, the young musim warrior Gahiji spoke with just a moment earlier. As seamless as a needle through cotton, the arrow struck the young man in the neck, through and through. Crimson blood poured immediately down his breast and erupted from his gaping mouth. Those around him simply stared with astonishment as the musim collapsed immediately to the cold, gritty sand.

While the lieutenant watched in total shock, he didn't see Gahiji handing him his bow back. Gahiji shoved it into the lieutenant's chest plate until his field liege clenched the bow.

Their eyes met. "Make camp," Gahiji said in a stern, unforgiving tone and stormed away.

∧∧∧

Osiris trembled at the presence of the large beast where once stood his brother, Seth. His long snout and ears curled in an uncanny manner. Half dog and half human waist-deep, Seth hovered over his sibling in bitterness and disgust. His eyes became mere slits covered in blood-soaked fur. He raised his sickled khopesh to the ethereal skies as one does a greeting to the stars beyond.

"You would betray your king?" Osiris muttered whilst prone on the floor of the ceremonial chamber. "Your

brother?"

*"It is you who has betrayed your people," Seth re-
sponded in his creature-like tone, void of humanity, absent
of compassion.*

*The darkness surrounded his very being, tempting the
silent whispers that echoed through the spiritual plane of
the inconceivable.*

^^^

The gathering was beautiful in a morbid skew of the
moment. Sorrow and joy competed for the hearts of all
present. Outside the ceremonial temple knelt thousands of
Egypt's citizens from every walk of life. In harmony, their
cries pulsated Napata's indigo skies with screams of remorse and fears of retribution from the gods. Under torchlight, mourners raised their palms to the night sky,
searching for answers to why they have lost their prince.

Within the dark, cavernous tomb beneath the desert
floor knelt the pharaoh, Piye. His long, graying hair contrasted with a mocha, Kushite complexion. To his liking,
the room was decorated with various shabtis, canopic jars,
golden scepters, and staves. There was a wooden figure of
Osiris, surrounded by scarabs and golden amulets. In the
center of the chamber sat the stone coffin, covered in religious texts and hieroglyphs. Within the coffin was placed
a child-size mummy.

Piye was a small man and once a crafty warrior. It was
him that unified the Egyptian Kingdom under Nubian rule,
earning the heavenly status as Beloved of Amon and the
Son of Re, as told in the Stele of Victory. Indeed, he had

scene death in the battlefield and souls washed away to the Kingdom of Osiris. As Rashidi began chanting ancient text to the twenty or so attendees of the funeral, Piye brushed his scarred forehead with a single, lean finger.

The year was 713 BCE.

Piye shifted his gaze to his right. There beside him knelt his wife, Queen Bahiti. They were both adorned in elaborate, lavender cotton robes with intricate golden jewels. "This is only temporary, my love. Theoris will have a proper burial. I am having a pyramid constructed in his honor," Piye whispered to her.

Bahiti remained silent and stared into nowhere. She wore a golden crown with a snake at its head and bird wings in full array. Only a single tear acknowledged that she was aware of the moment. After her six-month old son passed away in his crib, she had gone blind and spoke in gibberish only. In grief, she had shut herself off from the living. Bahiti was known throughout the kingdom for her beautiful, silky hair, even though she had worn braided wigs of late to hide her disheveled appearance. For a woman in her mid-thirties, she still maintained a youthful essence about her. Her miniature frame and unblemished Kushite skin complemented that fact. Piye had always loved his sister. Yes, his sister, a custom acquired from the original Egyptians. Keep the blood pure.

Piye placed a hand on her shoulder as the head priest, Rashidi, finished his sermon in ancient Meroitic. "I have Gahiji searching for the other heir at this moment. You have nothing to concern yourself."

Bahiti gave Piye a piercing glance. Her eyes were 11

glazed over as though looking through him. She returned her gaze back to the altar and coffin that held her deceased son.

Rashidi fell to his knees as another elderly priest banged a small drum rhythmically. Rashidi was a rotund man and who looked younger than his sixty years. Rashidi was a bald man with owl-like eyes, creating an uneasiness just to stare at the aging priest. As he walked to the coffin with a slight limp, the Kushite glared at the mummified child. He adjusted the belt on his priestly robe, and his eyes sunk to his chest. He stroked the frame of the mummy gently with his index finger. He admired the work he had done, the way he captured the boy's soul. He had washed the body carefully and proceeded to remove the internal organs, draining the child of all fluids. As he praised homage to Osiris, he removed the brain with a sturdy, metallic hook through the nostrils. Like a surgeon, Rashidi had sewn the body after filling it with herbs, spices, and wine. *Alas, Osiris will surely welcome the prince after my fine work.* He took one last look to ensure the canopic jars were in their rightful location.

The drum concluded.

Several ladies-in-waiting rushed in and slowly escorted the beleaguered Bahiti out the tomb. She sobbed with each step, muttering occasionally childlike rants of a babbling fool, a look unfitting a queen.

Piye stood as several servants scurried in to drape a feathered robe over his shoulders. Piye glared at his wife leaving the torch-lit chamber. He then faced Rashidi and said sternly, "Bring them in."

Piye stared at the mummy as several priest slowly slid the heavy, stone cover over his deceased boy. Atop the lid was a carving of the child that used to be, covered in jewels and lacquer. He would not allow himself to cry. He shifted his gaze to a deep ditch that dwelt next to the coffin. Several soldiers marshaled in a young woman and two small children, no older than five. Immediately, the woman fell to her knees and prostrated before Piye. The children cowered beside her.

"My pharaoh, I am with great grief and wish to accompany my prince on his journey," the woman cried as tears raced down her cheeks. "I ask that you please spare my children. The afterlife is not ready for their entry."

Piye took one knee and caressed her shoulder. "You have always been dutiful to my family. You earned your freedom yet have never left our side." Piye revealed a smile. "We must all make sacrifices for the Kingdom of Osiris."

Suddenly, a priest carried a torch and lit a fire pit adjacent to the boy's coffin. The combustible liquid inside erupted, warming the entire chamber and creating a menacing glow around Piye. He donned his hood. The white of his eyes penetrated the shadow covering his leathery face. He smiled.

"Have we not served the pharaoh well? I only ask that I may accompany the prince to meet with the gods," the woman pleaded, hands clasped.

"I see." Piye stood and stared the mother down with a stern glare. "I thank you for your service in this life and the next."

Piye exited his son's burial chamber for the last time to the screams of a family compelled to make their final sacrifice to the gods.

Chapter Two

Gahiji soaked in the warm bath, part of the supplies he requisitioned from the small village near Lake Nasser, including the teenage, Nubian girl that poured hot water continuously into his bath. Steam rose into the cold, night air, permeating his personal tent. His nude, muscular frame depicted the scars of battles won and wars lost. As the water trickled down the long cobra tattoo on his cheek to chin, he clenched the girl's wrist and stared at her sharply. The frail and nervous girl recoiled, nearly spilling the hot water in the bowl she held.

"Where are you from, girl?" Gahiji said softly with a smile.

"Sudan," she responded and then rattled off more words in her native tongue of Nobiin that Gahiji could not comprehend.

Gahiji released her and nodded for her to continue warming his bath. "Do yourself a favor girl. Learn to speak Egyptian. It may save your life one day."

She smiled and continued pouring.

His hair was braided but unkempt. The shadows created by the flickering candles danced back and forth as though they were alive. Alas, Gahiji began his diatribe as though speaking to the air:

"He will lead us. I truly believe that. Those who doubt

the fate of the gods doubt the very purpose of existence. They have no idea what the future holds for Egypt, my kingdom. How could they? Yet, they want to control my kingdom, my lands. Fools. The very existence of Kushites in Egypt would make the eyes of Horus blink. They believe they can control Egypt." Gahiji cupped the reflection of candlelight in his palm as the water trickled into the bath. "What they don't realize is that controlling Egypt is like controlling this candle's refection. The more you clench, the more it escapes your grasp."

Gahiji reached for his goblet of wine that sat beside the tub. He took a sip of the sweet libation. Indeed, he loved the fish but hated the river from which they spawned. He continued, "Death is upon us. Every man must reconcile with that fact. But he is a god? With Kushite blood? A pharaoh does not make him immortal in the eyes of Horus. He too will have his day. Yet, I still think of her, a spirit from the bright lights above. Curse him for intervening. Curse him for taking what is mine. It is a deep, and it is with great retribution. I will have what the gods promised me."

^^^

Piye entered the cavernous catacombs that housed the remains of pharaohs of the New Kingdom. The tombs were located beneath Jebel Barkal, a mountainous place of worship established by Thutmose the Third. The rocky structure was cylindrical and believed to be the spiritual source for the Kushites or Nubians. Just outside of Napata, the shrine was the origin of Shebitku's invasion of Egypt.

The inner chamber was filled with hundreds of candles that surrounded a muddy and shallow underground reservoir, filled with stone reliefs of past battles and triumphs. The queen mother knelt beside the pool, smearing mud on her face and chest. She was an elderly, Kushite woman of over seventy years, but she could have easily passed for much younger. She had ebony skin and a petite stature. She wore a braided wig and a ceremonial gown with embedded jewels. Tonight, she was barefoot to be closer to the gods.

"Your piety has me intrigued, mother," Piye said sarcastically.

The queen mother rubbed mud down her cheek slowly with her eyes closed. "The gods live in the mud, the stone, and the water. There is a branch of the Nile that leads to Duat. It is where Seth dwells."

Piye sighed and adjusted the belt of his tunic. "Do you offer any guidance when it comes to the Assyrians?"

The queen mother opened her almond-shaped eyes and gazed at Piye empathetically. "Sargon wishes to antagonize you. He is not to be trusted, much like his father. Do not let him goad you into battle."

"Sargon is a fly that must be swatted," Piye said adamantly.

"Perhaps," the queen mother replied. "He is a very large fly, Piye."

^^^

Chenzira waited until complete darkness before he would make his escape. It had been two nights, he estimated since he burrowed himself into the dune. Two nights of being submerged in the sandy coffin of the Nubian Desert, he remained. His only source of air was the small, thin, hollowed-out tree branch he used occasionally for diving for fish. He always carried the straw-like device on his person in case of a meal opportunity presented itself. Much like a sand lizard, he waited for the hunters to leave. They did not. So, he breathed intermittently through the tree branch, searching for oxygen. Above him dwelt the dead. The Kushites were there, lifeless, removed from this spiritual plane. Their bodies cooked in the glaring sun over the desert. As their bodies drained of any remaining blood, the sand soaked beneath them, often dripping into the face of Chenzira. The crimson liquid left a taste of bronze mixed with the bitterness of life's precious fluid as it flowed into his eyes and mouth. He had to get out of there. In an instance, Chenzira was taken back to the days of his nearly forgotten past.

"Do you take me for a fool?" the merchant shouted. His skeletal cheekbones quivered with great disdain and disrespect. The bony old man's frame barely held the extravagant, ornamental cloak symbolic of his class in Nubian society. His face maintained a shifty and murderous guise, cold-hearted from years in the dark alleys of Kerma.

Six Egyptian henchmen accompanied the merchant and three of them restrained Chenzira's father, a middle-aged fisherman from the slums of Kerma. His father appeared strong and sturdy but was beaten clearly short of remaining conscious. "No, my lord. If you were to give me time, in two moons I will have your gold," he muttered through his stubble-filled chin and cheeks. Both eyes were nearly closed from the constant pummeling he endured.

They were inside the shack of Chenzira's upbringing, a

below-modest abode with little furniture and dirty linen strewn across the blood-stained wooden floors. The dilapidated structure had never seen better days.

"Father!" Young Chenzira cried as he tried to break away from two henchmen in tattered tunics.

"Kill them both," the ruthless merchant said nonchalantly as he exited the shack.

Without hesitation, one of the henchmen unsheathed his small dagger and thrusted it into Chenzira's father. He bled profusely from his abdomen; crimson flowed to the floor below.

"Curse you!" the father exhaled as he collapsed to the moist floor. He gasped, hoping to avoid the inevitable. "Let my boy go," he said with his eyes shut.

The toothless henchman that stabbed him knelt over his near lifeless body while wiping his dagger with the bottom of his tunic. "You heard the man. I'm afraid the boy will go with you to the underworld." He chuckled and slashed the man's throat.

As Chenzira watched his father bleed out, he felt faint and furious, simultaneously. The three henchmen threw him to his knees. The tears trickled down his Kushite cheeks. Sorrow overwhelmed the thought of death. How could he live without his father? He was only twelve. He gazed at his dead father and noticed the pigmentation leave his father's flesh. No longer with the living.

"We'll take the boy with us. He'll be useful in the mines," the older henchman said. He was stout and grey, *although he was very muscular for a man of his age.*

Using his left palm, Chenzira dug a small shaft to allow his eyes to peak through the sand and espy his surroundings. He saw campfires with the silhouettes of musims about the encampment. There was the muffled sound of conversations and laughter as the warriors shared libations and stories of past triumphs. I must get out of here, he thought. His chest could no longer endure the pressure of the earth, and air slowly emptied from his lungs. He puffed the hollowed-out tree branch as his cheeks trembled with each clinch of his dry lips. Grains of sand permeated his nostrils, creating an itchy and painful irritant. Silently, he prayed for Isis to rescue her son and give him the fortitude of Horus. I will not let them take my eye! With that, he reached for the surface and grasped the cold sand to lift his wiry frame slowly and inconspicuously.

^^^

Gahiji let his bronze-hued fingers titillate the bath waters, occasionally allowing the liquid to stream down his muscular forearms. "Girl, who do you serve?" he shouted through his clenched teeth.

The handmaiden, who was cleaning a bathing pan, dropped the pan nervously and recoiled to the corner of the room. The teenage Nubian folded her arms as she crept into the shadows. Her eyes dare not meet Gahiji's. Alas, she was afraid, partly because the rattled girl could not understand what the Egyptian warrior was saying.

Gahiji grabbed his khopesh from the floor next to the tub. He unsheathed the elaborate sickle-sword from its scabbard. "Come here," he said in a deep voice. The chief

20

commander sniffled, and his right cheek twitched as though the cobra rose to life. His eyes became lifeless with the stare of unhappiness and duty to human nature, unavoidable duty to one's unforgiving and fateful destiny.

The young girl inched closer, timid with the fear one has when they step into an abyss, the unknown. She shook and her knees wobbled with utter fear coursing through her small frame. Motionless, Gahiji waited as a spider waits for prey to enter its web. As she entered his space, Gahiji stood, almost leaping from the water, revealing his naked, muscular body. The scars of past battles covered his bronze frame, like the heavenly bodies that dotted the midnight skies. He loomed over her with blade in hand. She cowered under intimidation.

"I once had two girls your age, not much taller than you," Gahiji said matter-of-factly. "In Memphis, they were its true beauty. Much of that had to do with my wife." His stoic stare soon transformed into a subtle, dare to say friendly, grin. Gahiji held the sickle-sword before him. "This khopesh is five-generations old, even going back to Esarhaddon the Untamed." He gazed at the weapon and admired its sharp edge and adornment of beveled jewels within its hilt. "Even though I was not there, I like to believe that if they were skilled in the use of such a fine weapon that perhaps…," Gahiji said as he ruminated at what could have been that night. The smile soon disappeared, and his eyesight found the girl once again. "Always arm yourself, girl, and be prepared to strike for you never know where your enemies will strike."

Suddenly, a musim of indistinguishable features, except that he was male and rather short for fierce warrior stock. The young Nubian breathed heavily and barely uttered his urgent message for his commander. "Sir, we discovered tracks leading away from the camp. It's him!"

Chapter Three

The Pyramid of Great Gatherings was the largest, most majestic structure in Napata, perhaps all of Egypt. It had stone blocks enclosed in bronze-plating, which glimmered from sunlight and moonlight at equal luminosity. Each opening into the magnificent fortress was protected by golden doors with two gigantic god-like statues guarding each entrance. Enormous stone-carved cobra statues ornamented its base, imposing an uneasy fear for those unwelcome or unworthy of their nightmarish presence. Every five paces stood a stately Egyptian guard in all regalia, day and night, their tunics woven from the finest cotton fields lining the Nile. Each wielded a spear of greater length than their muscular, battle-hardened bodies. Their cloth-covered headdresses instilled a belief in uniformity, honor, and to die for their pharaoh. As the sun rose from the Red Sea, Piye held a forum with his council of advisors and several dignitaries from neighboring regions.

The pharaoh sat at the head of the chamber in his bejeweled, golden throne. Piye wore his finest tunic for such gatherings. The embroidered, violet garb harmonized with his long, graying mane. Piye despised such gatherings, though they were required of him as pharaoh. He tapped his long, gaunt fingers on the armrest of the illustrious throne as he glared at the dignitaries seated on the stone floor before him on wool mats that provided minimal comfort. Torches lined the chamber's walls, and ancient hieroglyphs decorated the massive pillars providing stability for those within.

The elder from Rome spoke first. "You will find that Rome is a growing force, my pharaoh, and would make a worthy trade partner." He spoke in Egyptian with a tinge of an Etruscan accent through a full, grayish beard.

"The people are in good health, and the coffers are full, my pharaoh. Alas, there is the matter of…"

"We pay tribute to you, Pharaoh," the Numidian emissary proclaimed loudly. "However, our fields lack resources that…"

The voices blended. Piye was bored.

"We have much to learn from each other, Pharaoh. I ask that…" The representative from Greece said eagerly. His features were very porcelain and subdued.

How long must I endure? Piye was losing his patience. His thoughts carried him to the new stallion he looked forward to mounting. He had raised the illustrious Equidae from a staggering foal, the kind that never survives the unforgiving path of birth. He took a sip of wine and let the valley's fluid dance on his palate. Piye then flung the half-empty goblet across the stone floor. The metallic chalice made a piercing noise as it toppled and scraped past the men. "And what of Assyria? Sargon continues to haunt me."

"I believe they have garrisoned in Sinai, my pharaoh," Fadil said while standing in the corner of the dim chamber in his finest tunic of gold stitching. "We are to meet with their emissaries in Cairo in a fortnight."

Fadil was Piye's younger brother and shared his Kushite

blood. He was a very charismatic warrior for a man in his thirties, though his tight, mocha complexion and short hair gave him a youthful appearance. Being of tall stature made him a formidable warrior and chief advisor to the pharaoh and Egypt as a whole, although he was never comfortable with his height. *What woman would want a man so tall?*

Piye faced Fadil as the chief advisor fell to his knees and prostrated himself before his god. Piye gazed at his sibling as one does to a stain on fine cloth from whence you no not it's origin. "I see. Surely, you will be on your way, Fadil, yes?"

Fadil lifted his head. "As you wish, but will you address the rebellion in the south? The Sudanese are with arms and grow excessively."

Piye sat back in his throne and tapped the armrest with his bejeweled index finger. "Must I deal with everything? Get hold of your people, Chief Advisor." It was as though Piye held great disdain for his brother, his blood. He waited eagerly for Fadil's response. Piye's mouth was agape with anticipation.

They're your people too, Fadil thought but spoke with a softer response. "Yes, my pharaoh. I will squash their impertinence immediately. Blood will be spilt."

Piye shrugged and raised his hand. Quickly, an emaciated Egyptian boy, not more than twelve years of age, approached Piye and handed him another goblet and filled it with lavender wine. "So be it."

The twelve dignitaries present sat in silence until a Nubian advisor adjusted his robe carefully over his lap.   25

"Pharaoh, they are without. Perhaps, it would be better if they knew their protector was kind to their struggles."

Piye rose from his throne and took another sip of the purple libation. As he drank, a single drop trickled down his chin. His eyesight was never taken off the Nubian advisor. After a deep swallow, "Do not misunderstand me. What the people know bears little weight to me. I am concerned only with what they think. Set an example, and the lambs will herd, once again."

^^^

Later that evening, Fadil walked the torch lit halls of The Pyramid of Great Gatherings. He scanned the hieroglyphs of past pharaohs heroics, carved into the ancient walls. Even as a child, he thought of the structure as one large maze to entrap those who challenged Egypt's might. As he made his way to Piye's private chamber inside the pyramid's apex, Fadil contemplated how one exists in such a dark, cavernous labyrinth, alone from everyone, including a wife. He reached the door of the chamber where two guards in golden-hue tunics with bronze, chain-like armor held giant spears. They both bowed as Fadil entered the chamber.

The large, spacious room allowed for cotton bedding in the northeast corner with torches and candles illuminating the solitude afforded for such a retreat. The room lacked décor except for a jade-carved table with drawings of constellations and armor hung since Piye's past triumphs in battle. Fadil's espied immediately his surroundings. His view was drawn immediately to the opening in the ceiling, revealing the indestructibles, heavenly bodies such as the Big Dipper. The night sky was clear with starry pinpoints where the gods went about ruling mankind.

Right below the gaping square in the ceiling stood Piye. In complete nudity, the pharaoh gazed at the stars. Upon his shoulders slithered his pet cobra of the same name. The scaly creature moved about his frame as one does with a stone for sharpening their blade.

"Fadil, when we were children, we worshipped the Nubian gods. And yet, we now follow Osiris and his kingdom," Piye said. "Tell me, Fadil, are we forgiven?"

Fadil gave it too much thought. "I know not, Piye."

"One day, we will all be dust, and I will exist up there with the gods," Piye said with a smirk. He turned to his brother. "Until then, I am cursed. I have a dead son, an empire nearly at war, and of course, a wife that has gone mad. I am not forgiven."

"Your wife, our sister, is grieving, Piye," Fadil said with contempt. Fadil had wondered if Piye had forgotten that their sister shared their bloodline. Perhaps, it was a subtle ploy to aggravate his younger brother.

Piye stepped to the bedding and placed the snake down and donned a ceremonial robe to cover his muscular, battle-scarred frame. "Alas, Rashidi gave Bahiti the poppy. She now suffers blindness as well. What's a pharaoh to do?"

"Why did you call me here tonight?"

Piye returned Fadil's sharp tongue with a stark stare, void of neither anger nor compassion. He stepped before his brother with his hands concealed by the shimmering robe. "I should not be surprised. Weakness is in their nature."

Piye strolled over to the table and gestured to his brother to do the same. "I have another son. Gahiji is tracking him as we speak. Soon, he will return to his rightful place beside his father. No one needs to know he is of bastard stock."

"You send a beast to hunt a boy?" Fadil said with great concern.

"You do not care for the chief commander, do you? You mustn't let the past distort your judgment. He is very useful."

Fadil nods and releases an elusive smile. "Once more, the gods have given you the wisdom of the sacred ibis."

Piye pulls a rudimentary map of the region from under the constellation drawings.

"I will meet with the Assyrians in Cairo. Sargon should not take me lightly. He wants to trade with us, yet I know it is an invitation to war. I accept his deception." Piye folds the map. "You will rule in my stead. Squash the rebellion."

"As you wish, my pharaoh," Fadil said and turned to exit the chamber.

Piye gazed up at the ceiling opening, once again. He clenched his right hand as though squashing a supple fruit from the deep forests of the Nile Delta. "Fadil?" Piye said upon releasing his fist. "Do you fear death?"

Fadil stopped and said without turning his tall frame, "There are times that I do, but most times I convince myself to not be afraid of which I cannot control. Do you?"

Piye smiled and glared at his brother. "I am a god, or have you forgotten? It is quite a burden to carry for my people. I have decided to enact Stone Unguarded."

Fadil looked puzzled but decided to remain silent. He gave a tentative nod and kept walking.

"Fadil, do you know why I trust Gahiji?" Piye said from a distance.

Fadil paused at the exit. "No, Piye."

"He is loyal to the empire. Are you?"

Fadil's eyes met his brother's. "Yes," Fadil said as he departed.

^^^

In his dark, private chamber, many levels below Piye's, Fadil was practicing melee with his khopesh against a wooden pillar for such abuse. The sword chipped away at the cylindrical target with each blow. Fadil whirled and twirled to simulate combat, for which he had never experienced. Nonetheless, he struck as though to release overflowing anger that resided in his soul. Each strike gave birth to a grunt. His calloused hands were no longer safe from the havoc. Blood covered his palms. Perspiration poured down his bare chest into the crouch of his wraparound linen skirt. His biceps and pectoral muscles tightened as a heart pumps blood. Tears flowed from his eyes, creating a burning sensation with the sweat of his brow.

Fadil stopped swinging as the wooden pillar splintered away. His chest heaved back and forth in search of air. In his attempt to breathe, he gazed at his prized lotus flowers that sat in the middle of his chamber's man-made pond. The stony structure housed the violet perennials. The beautiful blossoms floated on the murky waters. Fadil treasured these symbols of rebirth as they rose from the mud each day. The portals of the chamber provided the necessary daylight for them to unfold. Alas, now it is dark, foreboding. They were folding for the night under torchlight, hiding their beautiful petals.

"Is this to be?" Fadil whispered as he wondered why his brother contemplated Stone Unguarded.

Suddenly, he heard the purr of his pet cat, Sheba. The African wildcat that Fadil raised as a kitten leapt into his arms. He dropped his sword to caress the small creature, stroking its soft, grayish fur.

"Happy moon, Sheba. How are you?" Fadil said with a large grin. The cat seemed to respond with a purr. "I can always trust in you."

Fadil sat alongside the pond upon the stone surrounding. "My brother is a testing soul, isn't he?" He said as he hugged the feline a touch tighter. Fadil then stared out an open portal and admired the constellations. "I will always love my brother and sister, although they betray Osiris. They are without heir. Will he continue to forgive them?"

Fadil kisses Sheba. "I feel I will never marry and enjoy the fruit of fatherhood. Your master is far too tall and lanky to attract a mate," he said with a small chuckle. The smile slowly dissipated to a look of disappointment. The corners of his lips tightened in face of his reality. "I am also a coward." He held tightly to Sheba.

The torches flickered into nothingness as darkness invaded the chamber. Sheba let out a piercing meow while leaping from Fadil's arms and quickly scurrying away. Fadil's gaze was drawn to the chamber's door. There stood a hooded, silhouetted figure, standing six or seven feet in height. The robed, foreboding individual stood in the shadows, not a feature revealed. Fadil's heart raced as he gasped then collected his thoughts.

"Why are you here?" Fadil said with uncomfortable anger. "It is not time. I am unprepared."

Chapter Four

"You cackling hens do this every morning." Abayomi brushed his dreadlocks to the side to see where he carefully laid the chicken feed. One hand carried the torch; the other held the bag of kernels. The Kushite boy was small which made him quick, so his mother had told him. His mocha skin lent itself to the harsh labor he did daily on the opium poppy farm. His uncle, Saabir, insisted that Abayomi feed their main source of sustenance each night before the moon reached the Hour of the Toad. Such tedious chores bored the twelve-year-old lad to no end. That night was especially excruciating since it was a humid, sticky night in Aswan village.

"You better eat your share. This is all you shall have tonight," Abayomi said to the family of chickens pecking near his feet. "Not you. You've had enough. You're the plumpest one here."

Abayomi stepped over the surrounding birds to avoid squashing the mindless creatures. He reached the small water troughs. They were empty. He slapped his tunic-covered thigh. "Son of Seth!"

Dragging his feet, he trekked to the barn and grabbed a pail from the wooden structure. The clank of copper against his knee drummed into the night air. Once he reached the stone circumference of the main well, he tied the elevated rope to the pail's handle. Using both hands, he lowered it slowly down, waiting for the splash. The pail stopped lowering, but there was no pail. Of course, he leaned over to determine the cause of the obstruction. His jaw dropped at the sight of Chenzira staring up at him. Chenzira braced himself against the walls like a crucifix spider in web, nearly ten feet above the dark waters below. He quickly raised his index finger to his lips, putting the weight on his calves.

Suddenly, Abayomi heard the galloping hooves of horses approaching the homestead forty feet away. Frantic, the boy dashed away from the well, dropping the rope and bag of kernels to the dirt. He was breathing heavily. "This is the worst night."

When he reached the modest abode, Abayomi saw his uncle exiting the home with a dirty rag in hand. "Uncle, I..." he said as four musims approached on horseback. They stopped. The neighing of their large beasts struck fear into Abayomi's essence.

Saabir wore a look of permanent disdain. Dressed in a grubby, cotton tunic and sandals laced to his knees, the scruffy-bearded farmer appeared as though the middle-aged man was still chewing that evening's repast. "It is quite late for a visit from his lord," he said matter-of-factly.

"We're in search of a young man of Kushite descent," one of the Egyptian musims shouted with his hand on the hilt of his khopesh. "We think he fled this way."

Saabir spit out the last seed of whatever he was chewing. He wiped his wrinkly cheek with his dirty backhand. He tried to remove any lasting fruit between his teeth with his tongue. "There are many young Kushite men in these lands. You are not far from Sudan."

"He is a lanky and quite crafty," the musim warrior said. "He is not native to these parts. You would have noticed him."

Saabir contemplated his hatred for the pharaoh with that of survival. It was a hatred that ran deep. Alas, it was born from the death of his sister. He had never forgiven what they did to her many moons ago. "Why do search for this boy? Surely, a god has more matters to sort out?" Saabir pulled Abayomi behind him and folded his arms. "Why are the pharaoh's men this far north?"

"Listen, Seth follower, you are not one to ask why. Simply tell me if you've seen a stranger in these surroundings," the musim said in a frustrating manner.

"As you can see, musim, I am not a servant of your false god. If I knew of this boy, I would not reveal his whereabouts to you or any of your kind," Saabir said as he took a step forward. Abayomi tried to grab his wrist to no avail.

The musim chuckled and dismounted. He smiled from ear to ear as he approached Saabir and brandished his khopesh. "It is true. All of you are repugnant fools."

He stopped to gaze over his shoulder at the war chariot fast approaching, leaving a trail of sand-clouds in its wake. "Yah!" Gahiji shouted while clenching the reins of the mrkbt. In mere seconds, he was upon them and brought his stallion to a halt. He removed his helmet and stood before Saabir some five paces away.

Gahiji nodded. "Good fellow, forgive us for disturbing you at the Hour of the Toad. We need your assistance as my men have unquestionably explained."

Saabir eyes were drawn to the cobra tattoo on Gahiji's cheek. He knew what that represented. This man had seen more than any man deserved to endure. Nevertheless, hatred fears only doubt. He chose not to be a coward at that moment. "My son and I are finishing our nightly meal." He turned to Abayomi and gave a quick wink. Abayomi looked confused momentarily as to why his uncle called him his son. "As I told your henchmen, I saw no stranger. Now, I request that you depart with great haste."

Gahiji stepped closer to the Nubian farmer. He placed his hand on the hilt of his khopesh. Gahiji sighed and stared amiably at Saabir. "I have many of my men searching Aswan at this moment. Perhaps, we will find him. We always find them."

"Is that so?" Saabir said with an uneasy smirk.

"That is so." Gahiji face hardened for a moment and then returned to a sinister smile. "If you would allow us to water our steeds, you would be serving your pharaoh with great honor."

"We have no water!" Abayomi said suddenly.

Saabir peeked over his shoulder at his nephew. "Yes, we can accommodate. Escort them to the trough, Abayomi," he said somewhat dumfounded.

"Ptah be with you," Gahiji said and nodded.

Saabir stared at the Egyptian with contempt, for he knew Gahiji was a follower of Osiris, most likely. The Nubian rubbed his gray pate and grunted as Gahiji proceeded to detach his horse from the chariot. The other musims dismounted and began following Abayomi slowly to the trough. Gahiji gave the opium poppy farmer one last glance as they made their way to the side of a weather-beaten shed.

"Boy, this trough would not wet one horse. Get more water from the well." Gahiji ran a single palm through the desiccated channel.

Abayomi nodded and grabbed a single pail and started nervously to the well.

"Wait!" Gahiji said over his shoulder while kneeling next to the trough. "I will assist you." He snatched another bucket nearby.

Dawn was quickly approaching. The horizon held a crimson and gold hue. A wave from the humidity rising from the scarce, desert landscape could be easily seen. Abayomi stood there, confused as to what to do next. He wondered had Chenzira made his escape while they had the cover of darkness. Gahiji walked by him, followed by the four musims after they tied their mounts to nearby wooden poles.

Gahiji was first to reach the well and espy the water supply. He leaned over and then attached the rope to the pail. Abayomi smiled immediately. He dashed next to Gahiji and set his pale down. He must have been smart enough to flee.

"Sir, why do you search for this common boy?" Abayomi said as Gahiji lifted the full pail from the depths of the water. "Is he a criminal?"

Gahiji shoved the bucket into his midsection, nearly knocking Abayomi to his buttocks. A dark shadow fell on Gahiji's bronze, leathery face. At that moment, he appeared very tall and foreboding to the Kushite lad. Without expression, he replied, "That is none of your concern, is it?" Gahiji lowered another bucket, lifted it, and then handed it to a female musim.

Saabir approached the two while the musims' horses proceeded to drink from the trough. Gahiji stepped away from the well to meet him. From Abayomi's perspective, he heard the muttering about the pharaoh and duty. He peeked over into the well. He saw a wet Chenzira breathing heavily in a crab-like position to support himself against the well's walls. Abayomi's eyes widened, and he quickly turned heel to face his uncle. He took a deep breath.

"Abayomi, carry the pail to the trough. Be quick about it," Saabir shouted.

"Yes, Uncle." Abayomi carried a full pail hurriedly to the horses.

After some time, Gahiji and his musims mounted their horses and chariot. He gave Saabir a final stare. "May Ptah carry you, farmer."

"May Seth give you peace, warrior," Saabir responded in counter while chewing on a small stick of ginger.

Shortly after the musims departed, a wet Chenzira sat on a pile of wild grass inside the dilapidated shed. There were no portals to allow for the bright sunlight that cascaded across Lower Nubian region. Only a single pit fire lit the humid space. He drank from a bronze container the satisfying liquid that once provided him with concealment.

Abayomi sat on the dirt across from him, tossing a single, large beet to the feet of a shivering Chenzira. "Would you like a blanket to dry?"

"No."

Abayomi nodded and stared into emptiness. "That is good. I am not sure I could sneak one past my uncle. Perhaps, we do not have one. The rains have not provided for the crops. I believe that my uncle has made Bastet angry and put a curse on the lot of us. The lot is him and me. He chased the village's cats away as if they are here to steel his copper or his crops. Of course, why would anyone?"

"Why did you protect me?" Chenzira said softly. Water dripped from his long braids, leaving small puddles of wet soil beneath him.

"I do not know," the twelve-year-old boy said as he gazed at the dirt floor. He seemed not to care that his only tunic rested on gritty soil. "How did you stay in the well for so long? You must be a warrior. Is that why they are looking for you?"

After his last sip, Chenzira tossed the copper cup to the dirt and started chewing on the reddish beet. It was delicious to his famished belly. He had not eaten in several moons to avoid his capture. "I do not know." He took another hunk from the sweet beetroot and devoured it like a lion at feeding. "I learned long ago that when soldiers are looking for you, you run."

Suddenly, Abayomi leaped to his feet. "Have you ever

been to Memphis?"

"Of course, I have." Chenzira said. He had not, but he felt the need to impress the lad, who was a few years younger than Chenzira only.

Abayomi's eyes grew bigger. A smile reached ear to ear. "Can you take me to this place? My uncle refuses."

Chenzira chuckled. "Why would you want to go there? It is a city forgotten by Duat. The filth that only a purveyor of lies would want to live is there. It is no place for a boy." So, he thought. "You are best-"

"My mother is there," Abayomi said in a panicked tone. "It was told to me."

"It was told to you?" Chenzira said with an arched brow. "Why would she be there when you are here? You speak foolishly."

Abayomi snapped his finger and reached in the pocket of his tunic. He pulled out a copper coin and handed it to Chenzira. "She gave it to me many moons ago when I was a child. She told me she had to go to Memphis and that she would return for me."

"When you were a child?" Chenzira said while shaking his head playfully. "Perhaps, you should await her return." He returned the Memphis coin.

"She cannot. She's now in the underworld with my father. My uncle has told me this much," Abayomi said with head down and rubbing the copper piece.

Chenzira understood what it meant to be without a mother and father, growing up in the slums of Kerma. They were taken from him without mercy, first by the gods, second by the scourge of humanity. He had to survive by catching fish in the Nile and selling them to local merchants. He was always a good fisherman, a trade taught to him by his father before he succumbed to libation and gambling. After his escape from captivity, he held on to the lie that they died in the last war between Kush and Egypt. It sounded more impressive.

"I must go." Chenzira tossed the remaining beet and stood. "I wish I could help you."

"I saved you." Abayomi grabbed his wrist. "You must help me."

Chenzira ripped his arm away. "I must live." He headed to the exit and was met with a surprise.

Saabir stood there with a sickle in hand. He stood there in astonishment and spitted out the ginger stick. "I heard some noise. Now, I know why."

^^^

Piye entered his merkhet, a chamber located at the apex of the Pyramid of Great Gatherings. The triangular-shaped room was decorated with bronze-hued stones with hieroglyphs carved from ceiling to floor. Torches lit the spacious chamber, revealing a single mat and a table covered with astronomical drawings of various constellations. He was followed by two barely clad men holding the bottom of his cape to avoid soiling the white, cotton attire. The slaves cowered as dogs protecting their privates. Piye stopped, and the two obedient men prostrated behind him, foreheads touching the floor.

"Send for my brother," Piye said as he gestured them away.

"Yes, my pharaoh," the Egyptian slave said as they both scurried out the room.

Piye had just returned from riding his favorite stallion, Kawa, the steed he rode in battle. The old horse could still run. He was wearing his leather riding attire with shin protectors. He removed the braided wig, fashioned from the wool of prized northern herds. His long, graying hair was in disarray. Piye pulled the torch that served as a lever to lower the eastern panel. The night, humid sky of Napata glittered before him. He knelt, gazing outward with his hands clasped. Orion was his focus, where the stars felt their brightest and Sirius could easily be found. The summer solstice was near.

"Osiris is omnipotent, benevolent to others, and my serenity. I know you sit beside him and grandfather, telling of your many triumphs, father," Piye said in prayer to Shabaka. "Yet, I feel I am at a disturbance, one that is of great consequence. The followers of Seth run rampant and seek to destroy what we've created. Alas, I am without certainty." Piye closed his eyes and gritted his teeth. "I've conquered Hermopolis and Memphis. I subjugated the would-be kings of the Nile. For many moons, I have ruled without hesitation and resolve. Yet, I sense destruction on the horizon. Father, the kings doubt me, and I fear it will come from within. What must I do?"

Piye was foreign to the thoughts of fear. He was fearless   41 against the Kushites, his own people, and the threat of the Assyrians. He did not like trials of the unseen. "Sargon has grown stronger in resolution. I know he is to be crushed. The Great Bear has spoken to me. How I long to be up there, by your side."

Fadil entered and took one knee. "Pharaoh, you sent for me?" He was dressed in his evening attire of a lion-skin robe and barefoot.

Without looking up, "Initiate Stone Unguarded," Piye whispered to his brother. Begin with Napata. Fadil, do it before dawn while they're in slumber.

Fadil stood. "What of the women and children, my pharaoh?"

Piye looked over his shoulder and stared sternly at Fadil. This occurred for an uncomfortable moment in silence. Fadil nodded hesitantly with a look of remorse. He exited the room, leaving Piye alone to consider the ramifications of his fear.

Later that dark evening, a family of four slept in pure harmony, unaware what was about to transpire. The young father put his two toddlers, a boy and a girl, to bed after repast. He was a pious fellow and prayed each night with his wife to Seth and Isis, opposed to Osiris and his mummy-like disposition. He was a local merchant of Napata, a trader of foreign goods. He gave his obligatory tribute to the kingdom and pharaoh equally.

As the moon rose to the pinnacle of the night sky, they were awoken by a crash. He grabbed the machete hidden carefully underneath his bedding and headed to the next room. He was greeted by Fadil and four Egyptian soldiers. Their white tunics reflected the moonlight in a ghostly way, each with a khopesh in hand.

"By order of the pharaoh, you are to come with me," Fadil said with an intentional, stern tone.

The father's jaw dropped, trembling and confused. He held tightly to the machete and stared Fadil's direction. He contemplated surrendering until his wife and children appeared behind him, obviously scared. He had to protect them. He founded misguided courage and launched himself their direction with blade extended. As if he practiced melee with a junior warrior, Fadil spun and disemboweled the father with one stroke. Crimson sprayed Fadil's face to the cries of the fallen and the screams of his wife.

Fadil sheathed his sword. "Take them away and burn the dwelling." He walked out the stone abode immediately and stared at the man's blood covering his hands. He did not want to take the father's life, but he was trained differently. He was trained to follow orders, regardless of their purity. His cheek twitched as the home on the outskirts of Napata crackled in flames. It occurred throughout Napata that night.

Chapter Five

Bahiti was supine on her embroidered, silk bedding, staring at the jewels embedded within the sandstone that covered the ceiling of her personal chamber. Sunlight penetrated the spacious, window-filled chamber as several handmaidens pranced around, performing their daily duties of cleaning, arranging, and such. She brushed her long braids aside and blinked from the dry air pervading the room. One handmaiden rushed over and helped Bahiti into a sitting position. She then gave Bahiti a small cup of warm water to sip. She did and returned the vessel to the elderly handmaiden.

"Summon the pharaoh," Bahiti whispered.

Later, Piye marched down the torch lit hallway. A bronze chest plate covered his leather tunic, and shin protectors were strapped above his leather sandals. He wore his kepresh, a cylindrical, violet helmet he often wore to battle. His small cape had a sewn image of a swift stallion with flaring nostrils. Servants lined the hall, prostrating before their lord, their god in Egypt.

"Bahiti," Piye said with a smile. "It is good to see that you are well."

"You are leaving," she said matter-of-factly.

"Yes," Piye said as he sat next to her, removing his kepresh. He caressed her hand gently. "Sargon must be dealt with."

Bahiti nodded. "Never trust an Assyrian, Piye. If he asks for trade, he is just delaying his ultimate motive. Perhaps, I will accompany you." She lets out a small groan as she attempts to leave the bedding.

"No. I forbid it. You must rest." Piye was concerned for his blood and wife. Although he held many concubines, Bahiti was the woman who bore him a child. It was a short-lived moment of happiness. However, he was told by the prophecy that his lineage would continue. There was another.

"Piye?" Bahiti said.

Their eyes met. "What is it, Bahiti?"

"I can see now. I can see everything," she said with a stoic expression.

"Yes, I know," Piye said a grin. "Rashidi informed me as much. He knew the poppy would work."

"You must understand, Piye. Now I can see."

"What do you see?"

She squeezed his hand. "I see you. Now, I see you."

Piye broke her grasp and stood. He was flustered, but he did not comprehend why. There was something mystic yet chilling in her voice. It was a voice absent of emotion or provocation. "I must go," Piye said. "Get better."

Handmaidens returned as he exited the chamber. Rashidi greeted him. The chubby priest stood there with his hands behind his back. His elegant robe and looped ear-rings dangling beneath his bald head gave him an appear-ance of aloofness. Spear-possessing guards lined the hallway.

"You said she was of better constitution!" Piye said within inches of the elderly man's face.

Rashidi bowed slightly. "My pharaoh, it is a matter of relativity. A fortnight ago, she was seen nude and speaking gibberish by interior slaves. Of course, they were immedi-ately dispensed of in-"

"My sister speaks as though possessed by Hathor. You swore by Osiris that you would bring her to health."

Rashidi thought it best to change the subject. "Will you be taking the Nile, my pharaoh?"

Piye took a breath. "No. I will travel by horse. It is time to remind the people of my might."

"Very good, my pharaoh. I understand you enacted Stone Unguarded? What is to be done with the Seth scoundrel?"

Piye rubbed his chin. "Sell them to the Israelites. They will pay a good share of talents for untapped labor."

"My sources told me there were unfortunate deaths in the process," Rashidi added.

Piye paused as he started to step way. "Make her well, Rashidi. You would be a fool to disappoint me again."

As the sun fell below the desert plains, Piye led a procession of 5,000 horsemen, 2,000 archers, and a full complement of auxiliary servants. His march started in Napata with the destination of Cairo. He stroked Kawa's mane gently as the horse trotted regally through Napata. Hundreds of citizens lined the roads, prostrating before their god. From an open portal in the Pyramid of Great Gatherings, Bahiti watched as Piye faded over the horizon.

^^^

Seth swung the khopesh and sliced off Osiris's left arm. Then he severed the right without mercy. His blood-red eyes and sharp fang dripped with the mucous of savagery. As his tail swung, he loomed over his brother in great satisfaction.

Osiris stood. Orion glowed behind him. There was no reality; not here, there, up or down. There were just unseen matter and the gases of star formation in the backdrop. With one intent look at Seth, the monstrous figure was repelled into the ethereal. However, Seth flew back with a screeching battle cry. Alas, he removed Osiris's legs and chewed on one for good measure.

"Your betrayal will be punished, Seth," Osiris screamed in divine pain.

"Osiris, it has already been rendered," Seth said while slicing off chunks of Osiris ruthlessly.

That day, the rains flowed heavily along the banks of the Nile.

Fadil knelt before the starry sky as the midnight zephyr whisked over his body and emotions, cleaning his soul from the doubts he wrestled to control. He raised his fingertips to his forehead while the chamber's torches flickered almost in unison. The devastation of killing a man weighed heavy on his conscience.

Fadil closed his eyes and asked for discernment. "Homage to thee, O Osiris, the lord of eternity, the king of the gods, thou who hast many names, whose forms of coming into being are holy, whose attributes are hidden in the temples, whose double is most venerated. Thou art the Chief of Tettu, the Great One who dwelleth in Sekhem, the lord to whom praises are offered in the nome of Athi, the Chief of the divine food in Heliopolis, and the lord who is commemorated in the Hall of two-fold Right and Truth. Thou art the hidden soul, the lord of Qereret-"

His cat, Sheba, meowed and leapt to the open portal's ledge, nearly falling to its demise. Fadil continued, "The holy one in the city of the White Wall, the Soul of Ra, and thou art of his own body. Offerings and oblations are made to thy satisfaction in Sutenhenen, praise in abundance is bestowed upon thee in Nart, and they soul have been exalted as lord of the Great House in Khemennu. Thou art he who is greatly feared in Shas-hetep, the lord of eternity, the Chief of Abtu, thy seat extendeth into the land of holiness, and thy name is firmly established in the mouth of mankind. Thou art the substance of Egypt, thou art Tem, the divine food of the doubles, thou art the chief of the company of the gods, thou art the operative and beneficent Spirit among the spirits, thou drawest thy waters from the abyss of heaven, thou bringeth along the north wind at eventide and air for thy nostrils to the satisfaction of thy heart."

He opened his eyes to a slight, ominous breeze that caused the chamber's door to open slowly. Over his shoulder stood the dark, robed figure, with his brow in shadows. Fadil took a deep breath and exhaled a white, translucent mist of vexation.

^^^

When Rashidi arrived at her private chamber, Bahiti had already donned her purple tunic, a gift from the despot of Phoenicia. It was embroidered with bronze pattern and an elegant breastplate. The ensemble accentuated her shapely figure. Her long braids were buried under a silk-woven wig with decorative jewelry the entire shoulder length.

"Prepare my escort. I will be departing at daybreak," Bahiti said while sitting before her vanity table. The dark eyeliner gave her a mystical character.

Rashidi cleared his throat. "My queen, the pharaoh requested that-"

"The pharaoh does not have to be concerned," she replied quickly. "I am feeling in better health. I am of great spirit."

Chapter Six

"I would have made gutted pig of him," Saabir said before guzzling another drink of northern wine from the copper cup. "At the Battle of Khartoum, I personally cut down ten Egyptians before the first arrow was launched. In fact, I served under Pharaoh Shabaka himself. That son of his is not worthy to rule, despite what the legends say." The three of them sat at the wooden table in the center of the dilapidated home for repast.

Chenzira stared at the contents of his plate, remnants of boiled bird, green leaves, and a baobab fruit. He nodded and ate the fruit in hand. The monkey bread was dry but sweet. He hadn't eaten in days but maintained the fortitude to remain free from capture.

"Why do they search for you?" Abayomi said while chewing the home-grown pheasant. "Are you a murderer? Or perhaps you are a thief? Did you steal from the pharaoh himself?"

"I did no such thing," Chenzira said.

"The boy does not have to have done anything, Abayomi," said a clearly inebriated Saabir. "If the pharaoh wishes you dead, so it shall be. I am no friend to the crown. Piye has lost his way and forgotten his people. One day, his reckoning will fall from the heavens. He is no god." Chenzira smirked as Saabir poured himself another fill of the wine from Sais.

"Still, you did not answer why," Abayomi said with a perplexed expression.

"You will have to ask them," Chenzira said while drinking water from his cup.

"How could you hold your breath so long in the well?" Abayomi said aggressively.

"Enough with the questions, nephew," Saabir said and faced Chenzira from his chair at the dinner table. "You are welcome here, boy. With a few chores around here, you can earn your keep."

"Yes, you can help me fish in the morning," Abayomi said eagerly. "I'm not very good, but I know there are plenty to catch. In fact, the shells are also-"

"I will help you," Chenzira said as they exchanged subtle smiles.

The Hour of the Hyena arrived, and dusk transformed the night sky to hollow black, and the desert plains howled with the cries of coyote in communication. The moist air clashed with the dry plains. There were occasional lightning flashes that lit up the horizon, shimmering off the Nile in wraithlike manner.

The mud-brick home allowed for an extra room filled with bedding, a lamp, and farming tools in storage. This is where the two boys slept. Abayomi curled on the floor alongside Chenzira on the straw-filled bed linen. Saabir had passed out at the wooden table, supported by inebriation and a sturdy table. Abayomi stared at Chenzira in the darkness. The moonlight that penetrated the space reflected off his back. As Abayomi watched, he saw Chenzira give an occasional quiver, a clenching of teeth, and the thrust of a spastic elbow. Chenzira was enduring his nightly nightmare. Abayomi decided against waking him in fear of being a recipient of his flailing in the wind. He watched and forced himself to close his eyes in bewilderment.

^^^

Piye led his cavalcade into the walls of the city-state of Thebes. The stone Pillars of the Great Hypostyle Hall stood nearly 150 feet and were the first structures to greet all visitors. Piye espied the Temple of Karnak, an illustrious and large edifice among many. The main cobblestone road gave Kawa's horseshoes a dramatic, pulsating sound as he rode the grayish stallion into the main square. Citizens, mostly commoners, lined the avenue by the thousands, all prostrating before their god and chanting.

"All hail the pharaoh!"

"All praise the great Piye!"

"He has come to protect us!"

The column came to a halt before eight men of noble descent. They wore long, silk robes, embroidered with the image of rams on its sleeves. Behind them stood a contingent of warriors in leather tunics and bronze chest plates. Each man carried a long spear, a symbol of their known ferocity. Piye dismounted and approached the noblemen.

"King Kashta, you were not at the gates to greet your pharaoh," Piye said to the middle-aged man of Egyptian stock with a single, gray ponytail that contrasted with his aging bronze complexion and rugged demeanor.

Kashta took a deep bow, followed by the others. "Forgive me, my pharaoh, my duties kept me from expecting your visit today," he replied.

Piye gave him a begrudging look and came within earshot of Kashta only. "I am obliged to cut you down like a rabid dog."

"Beg your pardon, my pharaoh, but you would not know a rabid dog if it bit you in your pretentious ass," Kashta whispered.

As though his face was a melting ice cube under the unforgiving sun, Piye's face went from frowning to a burst of laughter. "You were always an insolent bastard for eternity."

Kashta stood. The two men embraced with the affection of old friends. Piye gave him a subtle shake of the shoulders and they both chortled.

"It has been quite some time, Piye. You are well, I hope?"

"Osiris is always beside me."

The other elderly noblemen smiled in agreement of the moment. Piye and Kashta began walking slowly. Piye's cavalcade began dismounting from their steeds in unison.

"You are searching for answers to my presence here," Piye said with his hands clasped behind his back. It was a posture he often displayed.

Kashta gestured to the pharaoh to follow a particular path. "I am bewildered, yes."

Piye stopped and faced his longtime friend. "The Assyrians threaten our lands. They must be dealt with." They continued walking. "I am to meet with Sargon in Sais."

"I see," Kashta said. "I must insist that you and your men take rest here tonight. Sais is not far from here. Stay and celebrate in Thebes."

"You are very convincing, old friend." Have my men set up camp outside the city walls and give my personal guards run of the palace," Piye said as they approached the palace.

"When we learned of the prince, we mourned for seven moons, Piye," Kashta said for only Piye's ears.

Piye lowered his head and felt a moment of temporary sorrow. He had spent the last days erasing Theoris from memory. He had a land to rule and must overcome unforeseen obstacles, even the death of his infant son. *Why would Osiris take him from me if not for the prophecy?*

It was an awe-inspiring, ivory structure with stone pillars, two-story steps, and a vibrant fountain. The Statue of Anubis towered above a beautiful garden courtyard. Once they reached the top of the stairs, six guards in leather tunics and spears bowed at their arrival. The massive doors swung inward to reveal serene ponds dotted across the spacious room. Many men and women of nobility were in discussions and partaking in the local plum wine. They made their way to the inner chambers and stopped at a large, wooden door. The noblemen and guards who followed them bowed and left the two men.

"Do you remember we encountered those two alligators in Sudan?" Piye said and chuckled. "Who would have thought they could grow so big and fast? Did they not know there was a war to be fought?"

Kashta folded his arms and grinned. "I do remember watching you run and cry out like a lost goat."

"Indeed, I was not to be served that night," Piye said while laughing boisterously. "In fact, you will never convince me to hunt at night again."

Kashta laughed as well and grabbed the metal door handle. "We were young and foolish, my friend. Young and foolish." He stared at Piye. "Welcome to Thebes, my pharaoh." He then opened the large door.

When the door opened slowly, Piye looked like the feline that spotted its prey. Twenty nude women with statuesque bodies greeted him with appealing grins. They offered the variety he enjoyed. Some were imported from as far as Jordan, some were of Nubian stock. They were strewn about on luxurious furs and skins. Candles lit the chamber, giving it a misty and mysterious aura. Piye was pleased and grinned at Kashta while handing the king his khopesh and kepresh. Piye entered the room as the door closed behind him.

That evening, the main dining hall was engulfed in celebration. The forty-foot table, crafted from the tusks of African elephants, sat at the center of the illustrious banquet gala. Giant statues of the gods of Duat were at the perimeter of the airy, pallid chamber. Several local dignitaries, generals, and ladies in waiting surrounded the table while served wine and various fruits and red meat by captured male and female slaves from the northern battles. Conversations between the men and women were robust and filled with laughter and debate.

Piye sat on a throne-like chair on a platform just above the masses. Beside him were Kashta and three city-state officials of Thebes. All the men were dressed in ceremonial robes of the finest silk. A mix of Piye's guards and Thebes's warriors stood against the wall behind them, which displayed a large painting of Kashta dressed in royal regalia. Lutes and harps played melodically in the background. Piye took a gulp of his red wine and placed it forcefully on their wooden table.

"It has been too long my friend. My position does not allow for such joys. I miss the thrill of battle and the marches of tribute." Piye said to Kashta.

Kashta was inebriated slightly. "You have not seen the best part, my friend," Kashta said with an amiable smile. "I have something to show you. Do you remember the first time your father fought beside us in battle?" Kashta invited the officials into the conversation. "The first thing he told us was-"

Piye finished his sentence with him. "If you're going to fall in battle, be fair and allow them to join you!" They all laughed hysterically. "He was a man of pragmatism, indeed," Piye added.

Kashta nodded. "He was a man who carried the dream of a unified Egypt." Kashta clinched his lips and drank more wine. He looked sternly at Piye. "He knew that Egypt and Kush could be one, and he saw it through." Kashta rose from his chair and raised his goblet in praise. "Let it be known that Pharaoh Shabaka now dwells with the gods, yet he will never forget his people, servants of Osiris and defenders of what are just."

The attendees at the giant ivory table raised their goblets in support.

"May Shabaka carry us! May Shabaka carry us! May Shabaka carry us!"

"And may the gods continue to guide Pharaoh Piye, our great leader!" Kashta continued. "Although he chooses to rule from Napata, his blood runs deep in the sands of the Northern Kingdom. Alas, I was beside him as we battled our enemies of what used to be." Kashta turned to Piye. "Yet only a king is wise enough to silence his pride and fight for Egypt's greatest warrior."

The onlookers cheered; some men stood with their raised goblets. Piye returned the affection with a hardy smile and stood. He nodded to Kashta and waved the crowd and musical instruments to quiet down. As he gazed across the room, there was a moment of dramatic silence.

"People of Thebes, you are fortunate to have a king of bravery, resolve, and love for his land! Praise your king! Praise King Kashta!" Piye lifted his goblet to the cheers coming from those seated at the ivory table. "It is true. I rule from Napata, but my heart is grand enough to cover all of Egypt. It was a dream of my father's. He believed that when one is too far from Kush, he cannot stay connected to his true roots. He who does is condemned to the hells of an aimless void. This too, I believe to be certain!

As with Shabaka, it is my dream to create one Egypt, one people, and one purpose!"

Piye sat to further ovation and the harmonious music. Kashta leaned over and put his arm around Piye's shoulders. He took another sip of wine, which didn't surprise Piye. He could never out-drink the King of Thebes, even in their youth.

"That was beautiful," Kashta said in a whimsical tone.

"I'm fortunate you are pleased," Piye said with a grin then became serious. "Kashta, it is important that your warriors remain steadfast. Sargon may have other intentions."

"Let us not speak of Sargon or Cairo," Kashta said playfully. "You are here. The people can see you. Let us remember the days of old when two men challenged the gods themselves."

Piye looked sternly at his old friend and fellow warrior. His clenched lips altered slowly into a smile. He gazed into Kashta's eyes and drank from his goblet. "I must see to my men." Piye stood. "Keep my goblet filled and let us see who can endure the longest."

"Like old times," Kashta said.

"Indeed," Piye said and left the hall followed by his guards.

Festivities had ceased. The dining hall was empty except for the king and pharaoh. Each man had two personal guards in friendly conversation off to the side while Kashta and Piye carried on in brotherly banter. They discussed tales from battles to win Egypt, to bring unity to their respective fatherlands.

"The queen can be harder to command than the people of Thebes," Kashta said before grinning and sipping more wine. "How is Bahiti in these troubling times?"

"She is well," Piye responded. "To lose a child so early has not broken her spirit. She was always that way, even as a child herself." Of course, Piye did not believe the first words he uttered. "It is time I slept. We have a long march at dawn."

"Yes, age has betrayed us, hasn't it," Kashta said with a sigh. "Wait. Remember, I have something to show you. Come with me."

Piye nodded and they both proceeded farther into the palace. Their guards followed. Torches lit the dim passageways. The fortress was deserted, except for the occasional guard performing their duties. They arrived at a chamber's door. As earlier, Kashta created drama before opening the heavy door.

"Piye, this will be one for the ages," Kashta said with an affirming smile.

Piye nodded as Kashta opened the door. They entered the chamber, leaving Kashta horrified. Twenty of Piye's personal guards were standing over the bloody corpses of Kashta's men. In fact, the chamber's porcelain floor was layered in crimson muck. Immediately, Piye's guards behind them embedded their spears in the other two guards from Thebes, through and through. Blood splattered with their groans of mortality. Kashta was speechless while falling to his knees in horror. Piye stepped behind him and placed his hands behind his back.

"Kashta, I never told you about Cairo," Piye said between gritted teeth. "One does not become pharaoh without consulting with the gods. I have spies everywhere."

Kashta regained his feet and presented a small dagger from under his robe to Piye. In an instant, he regretted his transgression. *How could I betray my blood brother?* He wondered if his beloved city knew that his reign was coming to an end. Of course, Piye would never leave any rock unturned. Kashta's pride would not allow himself to beg for mercy. He would die a warrior's death and sit at the Grand Table of Isis. He shut his eyes and awaited his fate.

Piye had dealt with anger, fear, and defeat amid battle. These traits he could tolerate and overcome. Many times, he put his emotions aside and faced each one directly. Like the serpent that builds its nest close to the waters, let the sea do as it may. Reason over rashness was something he was taught by his father. *Stay focused until the war is won.* Alas, this was his first encounter with true betrayal. He had to ensure his sources were precise. Therefore, Piye learned of Kashta's dealings with the Assyrians from an ambitious chief advisor, loyal to the pharaoh. Kashta gave Piye the blade and discarded the top of his robe, exposing his muscular and scarred frame with a jackal chest tattoo.

"You were to assassinate me, Kashta?" Piye said. "Why? What did Sargon offer you in return, you bastard? Why would you betray me, your friend?"

Kashta opened his eyes. "It was for the good of the kingdom. Sargon made promises. I was just to hold you here. I was to keep you from the negotiations."

"But why?"

"Sargon wishes to avoid all-out war. You, on the other hand, despises peace. He understands that war will bring utter destruction to both kingdoms. Thebes destruction! I had to act," Kashta said sternly. "I would let harm befall you. I ask only that my family be spared. They are innocent in this, Piye."

Clenching the blade, Piye came within a foot of Kashta. "Innocence goes as far as one who decides it, Kashta. Fear not, I will not kill you this night. There is much to contemplate. Indeed, you will make amends another way. Remove him from my sight."

The guards ushered the king away, leaving Piye alone with his inner turmoil.

Chapter Seven

Lake Nasser flowed forcefully under the Aswan High Dam opening; a conduit normally closed to prevent flooding during the rainy season. The clear waters of the northern tributary reflected intense sunlight, serving as a conspicuous home for the school of Nile perch swimming below. Chenzira and Abayomi sat on the east bank that provided a high overlooking bluff. Abayomi was tying a string of silk to his self-created wooden fishing rod. While he was winding the string meticulously, Chenzira was discarding his tunic, leaving only his loincloth on to protect his privates.

"What are you doing? We're here to catch fish, not swim," Abayomi said as he applied the hook on the string.

"I'm going to fish how I was taught. Hand me your small dagger," Chenzira said while taking the knife from the boy. He cut a piece of the string and attached the dagger's handle to a stick he found on the dirty bank. After swinging his arms to get the blood flowing, Chenzira took a deep breath and leapt into the lake, stick and dagger first. SPLASH.

Abayomi stood and peeked over the cliff's edge. He was shocked that Chenzira dove a good ten feet. "He must be insane, an insane fisherman." He began to worry if Chenzira had drowned. It was at least six minutes before Chenzira surfaced with several perch impaled by his makeshift fishing spear. Chenzira reached the shore and climbed up the bluff. He started wiping water from his face.

"How did you do that, hold your beath for so long? Can you teach me?"

"It is just a matter of stopping your flow," Chenzira said as he sat and breathed purposely.

"Flow?" Abayomi said.

"Stop yourself from relieving yourself."

"Stop yourself from going there?" Abayomi said while motioning from his buttocks.

"Are you an idiot?" Chenzira said. "I think you are at times." Chenzira stood and removed the fish from the blade. "When you must piss your pants, hold it. It works for holding your breath longer."

"I want to try."

"Do you feel the need to relieve yourself?"

"No."

Chenzira sighed and walked to the younger boy. He took the tip of the dagger, grabbed Abayomi's hand, and poked his index finger gently. A drop of blood appeared.

"Ow! That hurt," Abayomi said as he recoiled and grabbed his hand.

"How about now?"

Abayomi nodded with a begrudging facial expression. Chenzira handed him the spear and gestured at the lake. "Jump."

After briefly hesitating, he did. It was no more than thirty seconds before Abayomi surfaced. He was coughing profusely, and saliva dripped from his mouth. "This is insane! You are insane!" Abayomi began wading to the shore.

"Wait. You must keep trying. It takes time."

Indeed, it took most of the day before Abayomi was able to spear a fish. He was so excited and simulated his spear-action for Chenzira.

"It was amazing. I could hold my breath longer. Seth's snout! I did it," Abayomi said joyously.

"That is amazing," Chenzira said in support of the boy. "Now, you can piss your pants."

Abayomi sighed as he relieved himself, unashamed by the fluid that filled his groin area.

^^^

Bahiti knew their stronghold was just south of Napata, in the desert hills of El Kurru. It was where they gathered to pay homage to their god, Seth. It was where rituals were performed to prevent the region from floods and the wrath from the god of chaos. He was a ruthless god that took his share of human flesh on occasion. Priests of Seth moralized murder for the sake of receiving purifications from the brother of Osiris, the slayer of kings and pharaohs. He was the chief deity of Upper Nubia.

"Stop!" Bahiti said to the six litter carriers.

Her litter displayed the wood-carved *heka* and *nekhakha*, the crook and flail of a shepherd over the chest of a warrior king. The gold-hued statue represented the pharaoh and his omnipotence over the land and its people. The small caravan was guarded by fifty armed Egyptian soldiers in white tunics protected by bronze pieces. Bahiti and Rashidi stepped off the large litter onto the sands of Kushite beginnings. They had made the trek rapidly, and the sun was at its apex. As the zephyrs struck Bahiti's small frame, she began walking towards nowhere, at least from Rashidi's perspective.

"My queen, you cannot walk aimlessly without proper escort," Rashidi said as he stumbled after her.

Bahiti stopped and looked for the landmark she recalled as a child. As she espied her surroundings, Bahiti took nine more steps and pointed to a dune twenty yards ahead. "There," she said to the line of soldiers behind her. "Dig into that surface."

Without hesitation or inquiry, the men rushed to the desert wall and started brushing the sand away with their bare hands. Eventually, the dune gave way to an inconspicuous wooden entrance of no peculiarity. Once the soldiers pried open the portal, they saw a staircase descending into darkness. Five soldiers lit their portable candles every warrior carried for night expeditions. They entered the subterranean labyrinth. Bahiti and Rashidi followed them. The stairs creaked with each step until they reached the bottom of the dark cavern. The dripping sounds of the Nile penetrating the earth could be heard. After negotiating the narrow pathway for two-hundred yards, the party entered a large, dome-shaped chamber. It was lit with torches and filled with fifty robe- clad disciples of Seth. The startled followers of Seth began displaying various weapons. The clangor caused the five Egyptian soldiers to unsheathe their swords.

"Wait!" the elderly priest said as he appeared from behind the followers.

He was a tall, lanky man of modest appearance. He was frail and supported himself with wooden staff. The elderly priest had a grey, bushy beard and unkempt hair. The lines around his sunken eyes showed he had seen years of unspeakable mayhem. He approached Bahiti with an uneasy grin.

"You will kneel before your queen, filthy commoner," One guard shouted as he raised his khopesh.

"She is not my queen, warrior," the elderly priest said. "However, she is a friend to the cause. For that, I offer my obedience, Queen Bahiti."

As the man bowed, Bahiti waved the guard to a posture of ease. "Akil, you honor me with your words. Surely, you are taken aback by my presence."

"Your beauty has yet to wane, Lady Bahiti. You truly are a site that is always welcome to this meager man," Akil said while regaining his stance.

The other priests of the Seth Order lowered their makeshift weapons of farming tools. The guards soon followed, and Rashidi stood beside Bahiti.

"My queen, you know this commoner?" Rashidi said after clearing his throat.

"He is an old friend," Bahiti replied and faced the head priest of Napata. "You would be wise to keep the pharaoh oblivious to this location."

"As you wish, my queen," Rashidi said cautiously.

Bahiti turned back to Akil. "I heard about the pharaoh's order. I'm sorry."

"Your husband wishes for our demise, always has, always will," Akil said with a sharp tongue. "He has forgotten the very people that put him in power, those who bled on the battlefield. My son died for Piye. Now, he will destroy us and himself in the process."

"I cannot show contrition for my husband's suspicions, yet I can protect the lives of your remaining followers," Bahiti said softly motioned a guard forward. He was carrying a sack over his back. He tossed the sack to the feet of Akil, and copper coins fell out.

"And what am I to do with that? Seth provides for us."

"Leave. Leave Napata before Piye's wrath causes further harm to your people," Bahiti said sternly. "It is but the rise of Ra before he returns from his travels and complete his ambition."

Akil chuckled. "Did I ever tell you of the story I was told as a child?"

Bahiti shook her head slightly.

"Once Horus matured, he demanded the throne from Seth. It was the throne he deemed belonged to his father. Alas, they battled for the control over all of Egypt. The boy was never a worthy adversary of Seth. He lost every battle until Isis came to her son's rescue. She was worthy and captured Seth." Akil stepped closer to Bahiti, nearly within arm's length. "In the end, she let him go, infuriating Horus to no possibility. Do you know why? She knew her husband, Osiris, should never rule Egypt."

Bahiti had a look of discontent.

"We must return to Napata, my queen. It is unsafe for you in this land at this Hour of the Hyena," Rashidi whispered in her left ear.

Bahiti gave Akil a final intense stare and began exiting the chamber, followed by Rashidi and the guards. It was then she questioned her presence there. She wondered if nostalgic memories of her father's pious friend distorted her judgment.

"May Seth give you peace," Akil said as Bahiti and her party disappeared into the shadows.

^^^

Abayomi and Chenzira began their long trek home, carrying their bountiful catch of the day. Dusk was upon them, and they were taking a narrow trail north through the hills south of Aswan. Abayomi was whistling as the two juveniles walked over the gritty path.

"Do you know whatever it is you are whistling, Abayomi?" Chenzira said with a chuckle.

"It is a song my mother used to hum to me as a child," Abayomi said.

"You still are a child," Chenzira said and stopped walking. Abayomi stopped. "Did you hear that?"

Both boys listened carefully until the sound of horses trampling the ground grew. Chenzira looked behind him. Abayomi hopped around in panic. The source of the horses' galloping appeared. The musims found them, led by Gahiji. They were a good hundred yards away.

"Abayomi, run!" Chenzira dropped his fish anchored on a string.

Abayomi remained still, confused. Chenzira sprinted a few feet and ran back to Abayomi. Chenzira grabbed Abayomi's fish and threw them to the ground. He shook the boy. Abayomi looked at him nervously.

"We must go!" Chenzira said.

"My uncle will-"

"Your uncle is most likely dead," Chenzira shouted. "How else would they know where to find us? We must go!"

They both dashed westward, cutting through the tall brush along the bank of the Nile. Gahiji spotted the two. He was on horseback as well, followed by all his warriors. He had to abandon his chariot to negotiate the narrow, mountainous path.

"There they are," Gahiji said with confidence. He whipped his horse to acquire more speed.

Chenzira and Abayomi maneuvered through the brush, falling at times. They reached the edge of a fifty-foot cliff overlooking a heavy rapid. The dark waters of the Nile rushed violently upstream, the remnants of an open dam.

"We have to jump," Chenzira said frantically.

"Why do I have to jump? They are looking for you, not me," Abayomi screamed.

The musims were forty yards away. Gahiji felt the anticipation. The search was over. He yanked at the reins to guide the horse through the heavy brush.

"Do you have to relieve yourself?" Chenzira said as he saw the horsemen approaching quickly.

Abayomi nodded.

Instantly, Chenzira grabbed Abayomi by the shoulders, gave him a final stare, and tossed him over the edge. Abayomi screamed obscenities as he plummeted into the raging waters. Chenzira said a quick, silent prayer and joined him. They both disappeared under the river current as Gahiji dismounted and gazed over the edge. The other musims dismounted and stood beside him.

"I doubt they could have survived such a fall, Chief," one musim said.

Gahiji stared at the river and clenched his fists. His cobra tattoo began to tremble. He did an about face and mounted his horse. As the steed began neighing, Gahiji looked at the musims.

"We return to Napata with the boy, or none of us returns," Gahiji said as he galloped away.

Chapter Eight

When Piye arrived in Cairo, he was greeted by its inhabitants and Alara, the Nubian king appointed by Piye. Thousands prostrated before him as he rode in on Kawa like leader of a pride of lions. Tantara played throughout the beautiful city at Piye's arrival. The center of the walled city contained structures with stone spires that seemed to reach into the heavens. As his procession of cavalry entered the citadel behind him, Piye espied the illustrious city-state and thought he must raise their taxes. Piye dismounted and was greeted by King Alara and his followers.

"Welcome to Cairo, my pharaoh. The conference awaits your eternal wisdom," Alara said as he stood and bowed dramatically. He was a bald man of short, muscular stature. Also, he was a youthful king, which really bothered Piye, tremendously.

Piye stepped around him in silence and continued walking to the main fortress, a pallid, stone stronghold surrounded by a hundred Egyptian spearmen. He never cared for Alara. He appointed the war-like ogre to appease his wife, Bahiti. The two were childhood companions in Napata. The stoic pharaoh's thoughts were within the walls before him. Like a wizard conjuring spells, Piye was eager to see the outcome of his ruse. He walked up the fortress's spiral staircase as he discarded his ceremonial cape for the servants to pick up. However, his kepresh remained, along with his cotton tunic with embroidered designs of wolves. He entered a large chamber with ten men kneeling on each side of a violet, twenty-foot rug. Piye sat in a raised throne at the end of the rug. Ten of his personal guards stood behind him. After the men finished bowing, they raised their heads. Piye saw five Egyptian diplomats on the left and five Assyrian emissaries on the right.

The lone middle-aged, Assyrian woman of no beauty or intrigue knelt in the middle of the two lines. She wore a satin, red dress and tied hair in a bun. Her face was hidden subtly behind a translucent veil.

"Leader of Egypt, we are most pleased with your arrival. However, we were expecting King Kashta in your stead. I am Athra, the chief diplomat for the great Sargon, the god with us and Lord of the Furthest Reaches," she said as if chanting.

"And I was expecting Sargon himself, not some woman to address me," Piye said as he folded his legs and leaned to the side while sighing. "However, the fact that you speak our language is commendable."

"Yes, Pharaoh Piye, you will find I am skilled in multiple languages. I am also fluent in several dialects of Meroitic," Athra responded amiably. "My forgiveness, we were under the assumption that you were preoccupied with other immense duties. Might I ask if King Kashta will join us soon?"

"He is preoccupied with other immense duties," Piye said sarcastically. "What does Sargon want from me? I thought he would be busy dealing with the Philistia uprisings."

"He wishes to express his interest in opening trade between our two lands. It is a very nice arrangement; one we

73

share with Iberia. I believe you will find it very favorable to the Egyptian people."

Piye chuckled and stood. He stepped down from the raised platform and came to within inches of Athra. He knelt to face level of the Assyrian. He never looked more serious than that moment.

"I have a message for Sargon," Piye said. "I also feel it will be most favorable to him and his people." He pulled down Athra's veil forcefully. Her face held a certain attractiveness of soft eyes and hard features. She had an almost divine beauty found only in mythology. "You tell Sargon, that if one ship enters the Mare Internum or a cart enters into Sinai, I will consider it an act of war."

Athra was stunned, unable to speak. She watched as Piye, his diplomats, and his guards departed the chamber in haste. It was a brief negotiation. Athra faced the other emissaries.

"Sargon will not be pleased."

^^^

Rashidi separated from Bahiti and continued south to Meroe. It was there, the Pyramid of Theoris, where Rashidi had to perform his ritual duties. The village was scarcely populated. He rode there by horse-driven wagon. Sweat trickled down his brow to his chubby cheeks. He despised the humidity at that time of night. The Nile flowed by as Orion guided his driver through the desolate hills. Once he arrived, he was greeted by his most trusted priest.

74   "Has the cargo arrived?" Rashidi said.

The robed priest nodded. He was pale and had painted eyelids and marks of obedience on his face. If the priest did not clear his throat occasionally, one would have thought the young apprentice was a walking corpse. The frail Egyptian priest followed Rashidi to the massive pyramid that was constructed of heavy stones and copper. Nearly ten-thousand slave laborers built the final resting place for Theoris at the behest of Piye. The pharaoh would ask Rashidi to also honor his son in another way.

On the first level, a small pony stood in a murky, spacious room. The *ibw* was bare of decorative or ritualistic décor. The pony was chained to the stone floor at each hoof. Its neck strapped to a cylindrical stone, restraining the mount's movement. The pony neighed in constant fear. The chains rattled with each movement. Rashidi discarded his ceremonial robe. He unsheathed a long dagger from the belt of his tunic. The blade had a hilt of copper and was sharp on one side. With the young priest, both pious men began chanting ancient hymns to Osiris with their hands over their chests. Upon finishing, Rashidi inserted the blade into the pony's throat and worked the dagger from ear to ear. Blood flowed from the beast as it screamed its final cries for help. The blood dripped to the floor until the pony collapsed and ceased breathing.

"Let us prepare the gift from the pharaoh," Rashidi said nonchalantly.

Rashidi and his apprentice detached the chains from the floor anchors and attached them to a lever apparatus. Together, they pushed down on the lever, elevating the pony upward by its legs. As the crimson blood continued to drain, Rashidi cleaned the blade of its impurities. He started removing the pony's entrails, the lungs, heart, stomach, liver, and intestines. The odor was repulsive yet familiar to the head priest. He moved on to the brain cavity, removing the brain carefully through the nostrils. The apprentice placed the organs in canopic jars, except for the brain. It was tossed aside. The jars were placed in a chest decorated with four images of the sons of Horus. Then they rinsed the carcass with buckets of water, wine, and various spices. Satisfied, they stuffed the pony with mineral salt. To complete the process of dehydrating the body, they rubbed more salt over the entire pony. They then sat in prayer. There were only four ponies left to purify and place beside Theoris.

Rashidi thoughts were swept to the days of his capture by the Seth Order as a child. It was the first invasion by the Kushites. The reason for his limp resurfaced. The followers carved his toes on his right foot for an archaic ceremony. Rashidi had considered if they planned to chop off more as that brutal night could have panned out. After the monstrous disciples slaughtered his entire family before him, they decided to keep Rashidi alive as their sniveling slave, to serve their carnal desires. He knew that the single purpose to continue living was the complete destruction of the sect.

"What we sacrifice today will return to us in great multitude," Rashidi promised himself.

Chapter Nine

Fadil visited the open market often when he wasn't sparring to improve his melee skills. It was a cloudy day in Napata. The city square was robust with people from all corners of the kingdom. Women and elders bartered with a variety of shopkeepers selling their goods, from eclectic spices to expensive garments weaved from other lands. Palm trees dotting the brick avenue provided unnecessary shade. Fadil wandered the market wearing a modest tunic with a cape and his khopesh, revealing his military status. Occasionally, a passerby saw who he was and paid homage with a slight bow. Fadil acknowledged them and moved on.

A dark-haired woman with bronze complexion and almond-shaped eyes caught his attention, though he pretended it was what she was peddling. He approached the statuesque, young lady in gown in a slouching manner. He was subconscious about his height and tried to make himself less intimidating.

"What are these?" Fadil said with a smile.

She reciprocated his genial greeting. "These are the finest fragrances from the royal family of Veneti," she said with an unfamiliar accent.

"You are from there?" he said as other patrons left them alone for the other tents.

"No, I am from Sicilia," she replied as she chose a small

flask of blue liquid. "My father imports many things from far away. Smell this." She placed the perfume under Fadil's nostrils.

Fadil inhaled subtly, and the whiff gave him a floral scent. "It is very nice but not to my interest."

"Perhaps, your lady-friend will find it intoxicating, no?" She said as she placed it on the small, wooden counter in front of her.

Unwilling to reveal the truth and divulge his lack of courting experience, Fadil nodded. He grinned and held the flask to his nose once again. "Do you find it intoxicating?"

She shook her head. "No, such a fragrance surpasses my status in the land. I prefer a more subdued aroma," she said with a smile while squinting.

Fadil studied her opal eyes and shapely figure. In his eyes, she was beautiful in a mysterious, playful way. Her modesty only fascinated the malleable warrior. He was captivated by a passion he had never felt.

"What is your name?" Fadil said.

"I am Catena."

"That is beautiful. Is it taken from your mother?"

"No," Catena said as she shook her head while blushing. "My father says he chose my name for the survival of our people."

Fadil's brow wrinkled. He tried to decipher what she

said to no avail.

"It is an old Etruscan tale in which the gods will send someone to unite the people of Etruria to defeat the malevolence. That person will be known as Catena," she said softly.

"That is quite a tale," Fadil said with a nod.

"And your name is?" Catena said with a shifty smile.

"Fadil."

"Well, Fadil, are you a warrior?"

"I am. I fight for the pharaoh."

Catena gave a look of contemplation and started walking away.

"What is it?"

She paused. "I lost three brothers in war. Each time my father would say, 'How did I rear three children to sacrifice everything for a king who would not return such favors?' He saw it as foolishness."

Fadil was offended by her comment. He folded his arms in protest. "Is it foolish to sacrifice for your bloodline? I think not."

"I did not mean to offend you, Fadil," Catena said. She gave a forced smile. "It was just something my father had to tell himself to overcome the guilt he must have felt." She began setting more flasks on the counter, appearing to shift her focus away from Fadil.

Fadil raised his index finger to retort, but he was left without a logical way to respond. Did she not know he was royalty? However, there was part of him that thought she might know exactly who she conversed and held no apprehension.

Fadil tossed two coins on the counter. "I will purchase the blue fragrance."

^^^

Abayomi dove into the darkest regions of the Nile and speared several fish while there. Each time, he increased his ability to expand his lungs' capacity to provide necessary time to hold his breath, thanks to what he learned from Chenzira. It was chilly as dusk set in on the eastern bank of the Nile. They made camp a few miles north of Aswan.

"Where is the fire?" Abayomi said as he walked up the small embankment, water dripping from his loincloth.

"I told you before that it will attract the musims to our location," Chenzira said as he gathered leaves from nearby sycamore fig trees to construct makeshift bedding. "Besides, fish taste better uncooked."

"That cannot be good for your insides." Abayomi laid the fish on the sand and sat cross-legged. "My uncle told me to always add fire to your food. He would never-"

"Well, he is no longer of this land, most likely," Chenzira responded with exasperation. "I am going to relieve myself."

Abayomi threw his fishing pole down and watched Chenzira walk away into the river's shrubbery. He wiped the grit from his face and lowered his head, partly from exhaustion. He was saddened by leaving his uncle behind, his only connection to his mother. He bit into a raw perch and immediately spat it out.

As Chenzira urinated off the small embankment, he watched the sun disappear into the horizon. The sky was a burnt ginger hue, and the mating calls of African sacred ibis permeated his surroundings. "I have to rid myself of the child," he said with a smirk. In fact, he began to chuckle to himself. "Chenzira, they will never take you back. You will always outsmart the Egyptian fools." He stopped chuckling when he heard the honks increasing in sound and proximity. He espied the dark brush until he found the source of the sounds. He tumbled to his buttocks and dashed the opposite direction.

Abayomi lifted his head to the heavy cracking of brush and twigs. He stood up and saw Chenzira running his direction. He squinted in hopes of finding reason for his fellow traveler's panic. Chenzira was within twenty feet of Abayomi.

"RUUUUUUN," Chenzira screamed as he flashed by Abayomi.

Abayomi's confusion changed quickly into utter fear as a female hippo charged his direction. He did not hesitate to follow Chenzira. "Son of Seth!" The hippopotamus was quick on her feet for her size.

The hippo was gaining ground. He was in danger of being trampled by the beast and bitten. His instincts took over. Like a villager gathering fruit for repast, Abayomi scaled a large fig tree in seconds. He accomplished this feat with bare limb and uncontrolled adrenaline. As his heart thumped hysterically, he gathered his breathing and began exhaling with some normalcy. Abayomi watched the hippo let out a few more honks before returning to the comforts of her river dwelling.

A few minutes passed before Chenzira appeared below him at the bottom of the tree. "You, okay?"

"You left me!" Abayomi said as tears rolled down his cheeks.

Chenzira focus was on the river. "I did no such thing. I am right here. Get down from there," he whispered, afraid of signaling the beast, once again. "We must continue moving."

Abayomi slid down the tree as though it was a wet pole. "I do not care. I am going home. How foolish it was to follow you."

Chenzira gestured for Abayomi to leave. "You can leave. What do I care?"

They both started marching opposite directions until Abayomi reconsidered his departure. He wasn't sure of the path home, at night especially. Before losing sight of the wiry Chenzira, Abayomi raced to catch up with him.

Darkness enveloped the hilly landscape. The appearance of multiple torches gave them pause. Both boys were lying supine behind a large boulder as the caravan of horses and wagons trekked along the eastern shore of the Nile. It was Piye returning from the northern plains. Like a bronze and purple peacock, Piye sat atop his stallion while evoking confidence and rigidity. The moonlight provided adequate luminosity to guide him home to Napata.

Chenzira rolled over and peeked around the stone to glimpse the horse procession. "It is the pharaoh on the march," he whispered.

Abayomi looked puzzled. "That does not concern me."

"It should. Who do you think those hunters work for?" Chenzira said as he rolled back on his posterior. "We will wait till they pass."

Abayomi rolled over and stared at Piye. He saw a hardened warrior leading hundreds of soldiers, if not thousands. Abayomi wondered why the pharaoh would search for Chenzira and why he was to be feared. His uncle told him that the pharaoh was a failure to his people and should find the happy end of a sword. For a second, it appeared that Piye looked his direction. Abayomi panicked and cowered quickly behind the boulder, once again.

"I think he saw me. The pharaoh saw me."

"Do not be a fool. No one can see in the darkness," Chenzira whispered while peeking again.

He watched as the cavalcade continued their journey.

Chapter Ten

Piye reached Napata by dawn. He did as he often did each morning before he held court. He was riding Kawa in the courtyard of the Pyramid of Great Gatherings. In his riding equestrian clothing, he guided the horse through the large, interior field, over obstacles built specifically for his enjoyment. Piye executed the highest hurdle last. Kawa had to clear a four-foot pole, a feat the horse accomplished on numerous occasions. After making the last jump, Piye escorted Kawa to his private stables that housed ten of his finest breeds. It was time to reign.

Piye changed into his royal garb of white, silk tunic, cloak, and his ceremonial bejeweled kepresh. In his immaculate throne room of golden stone carvings and large statues of various Egyptian deities, he governed. He shifted from side to side on his throne of stone, wishing for the day to come to an end. Village elder after village elder pleaded for more funds to replenish their water sources and other sustainability projects. So, he sat there, showing little interest and brushing aside one commoner after another. Once he gave his verdict, his ten personal bodyguards would simply escort the frustration out the enormous chamber. Until finally, his wish came true. Besides the bodyguards, Rashidi, Bahiti, Fadil and his mother remained.

Piye sighed. "Egypt would be a more delightful place if weren't for its dwellers," he said while removing his kepresh.

"You must be very fatigued, son. Perhaps, you should rest," Piye's mother said.

"Pharaoh, the people spirits are low. I fear great disdain for the future," Rashidi said as he stepped forward and bowed.

Piye stood and removed his cloak. "Leave us."

The bodyguards left the chamber in single file. Piye approached a small shelf nearby that housed a khopesh, once held by Shabaka. He admired the blade, its jewel-encrusted hilt, and its lightweight balance. It was the perfect tool for killing.

"Fadil, I understand you had to shed blood in Napata?" Piye said as he stared down his brother.

Fadil stepped forward. "Yes, brother, I had no other choice in the matter. I had to kill in your name."

"And you made that peasant a martyr? They were to be sold as slaves. Yet, you could not follow that simple command!" Piye placed the blade back on the shelf. "I was told they are marching in the streets, shouting disparaging remarks about their pharaoh, their god!"

Bahiti was about to speak on Fadil's behalf, but his mother cut her off. "You ordered Stone Unguarded. Did you expect a different consequence?" she said with a snicker.

"You are correct, mother. Only a fool would send an idiot to do his bidding," Piye said stoically. "I try to ignore that my brother lacks ordinary sense. You were always the weaker of us. The day will come when I will no longer protect you from your errors and wicked ways."

Fadil was unresponsive. He did not defend himself or give an argument. As usual he sulked under the brutal words of his sibling. Fadil withheld the anger that roared in his limbs. For a moment, he thought of the unthinkable. However, Bahiti would protest on his behalf.

"Piye, have you forgotten? We shared the same womb. You are not without burden when dealing the Seth followers," Bahiti shouted.

Piye shifted his sight to her. He moved closer to her. They could have kissed as husband and wife. Instead, they squabbled as brother and sister. "And you, you undermine me at every moment. Did you not think I would hear of your assignation with the priest? By Osiris, I should have your head!"

She looked directly in his eyes. "You could, Piye, but you haven't the yearning."

Piye stepped back and touch his forehead in frustration. "I only want what is best for Egypt, our family. I have barbarians in the east, insurrectionists from the south, and tribes from the west! It is but the mercy of Isis that I remain sane. Can you not step into my light? The Seth believers desire only to inflict havoc and destroy what I built."

"Your father also wanted the best for his family and kingdom. In the end, he allowed the accolades and cheers destroy him. He had forgotten the way of the Kushites, the way he won Egypt," his elderly mother said softly. Under her gray braids was a very soft, youthful expression. The petite woman had a persona of peace and sorrow, simultaneously.

Piye gave himself two seconds to reflect on her words before lashing out. "I am pharaoh. I am a god." He sat on the throne. "You would be wise to remember, mother."

Rashidi felt the tension in the chamber and decided to intervene. "My pharaoh, I suggest we hold games to uplift the spirits of the people. They yearn for a departure from the despicable Seth filth. I suggest a chariot race in your honor, here in Napata."

Piye rubbed his chin. "Yes, the people need a distraction. Perhaps, a race to memorialize my victory over Tefnakht would suffice? I shall enter my finest steed. Let the commoners know."

"Yes, my pharaoh," Rashidi said graciously. "May Osiris carry you."

"May Seth give you peace," Bahiti said under her breath as everyone departed, leaving Piye alone on his throne.

^^^

Osiris gasped for the heavens as he espied his body parts strewn about the palace floor. A brother's betrayal was without mercy. As he took his last breath, he speculated whether the price that came with ruling Egypt demanded complete destruction of the body, of the soul. The clouds merged like to horned creatures clashing on a hillside. Thunder erupted over the lands and heavy rain drenched the sands of Egypt. All was lost until Isis arrived and knelt beside her beloved husband.

87

"Great sorrow, Osiris, has engulfed my heart. Perhaps it is time for your long sleep though you cannot die," Isis cried to the ethereal plane. "You must not perish at the betrayal of your cowardly brother, for he will feel my wrath. I honor the dead and prepare them for their path to the underworld. They are not worthy of Duat, my love. You are pharaoh. Such a place only waits for your sort. I am with child, and you must be there as father. You must be there as king of Egypt."

Isis caressed his temples. She began her incantations and clenched her eyes. The winds of enchantment surged over Osiris, breathing life into his lungs. Each body party appeared to crawl back to their rightful place as one. Once again, Osiris was one body, a soul, and a king.

"Seth must face retribution for his malevolence. His jealousy angers the gods and intrudes on their fortunate foretelling," Osiris said as he stood and adjusted his tunic. "You did well, wife. Now I must find Seth. You will cloak me in bandages from your deepest reaches and give me the advantage of the unexpected. I will deal with my impertinent brother."

Chapter Eleven

Catena and another young woman of Sicilian lineage were dismantling their tent from which they sold their imported fine goods at the open market in Napata. As dusk set upon the horizon, six Egyptian horsemen arrived abruptly. Their steeds galloped within feet of the two startled women. One of the horsemen dismounted and handed Catena a scroll.

"My papers are current, sir. I have the consent from the constable to share my goods here, each day," Catena said nervously as she unfurled the scroll. A flask of blue liquid fell into her small palm.

"Your presence is requested at the Pyramid of Great Gatherings by the chief advisor to the pharaoh at the Hour of the Toad, a fortnight from this day," the horsemen said as sternly and as stoically as possible.

The horseman mounted his neighing horse quickly. The cloth that covered his head fluttered in the breeze. "I was told to instruct you to wear that fine fragrance on that day."

He whipped the reins, and the entire group of horsemen was gone with clouds of smoke at their rear. Catena and the other woman exchanged looks of astonishment as a few onlookers gossiped as to what they just witnessed. Catena was able to read the scroll and saw the mark of the pharaoh. Egyptian was her second language of five. The other woman smiled.

"There are two kinds of powerful, too much or none at

all," Catena whispered.

^^^

In the mountains south of Thebes, Chenzira's thin frame shivered in the night, not from the elements but from his persistent nightmares. Abayomi stared at him from his palm-leaf bedding. Their small campfire ceased to burn and left smoky embers only. They made camp next to the palm tree to divert the smoke up its shaft and out its apex. This was Chenzira's idea to conceal their location. The scent of wild beasts and buzzing insects permeated their surroundings.

Abayomi sat up. "Chenzira, do you hear that? Chenzira, do you hear that?"

"No," Chenzira responded without opening his eyes.

"I have to find my mother," Abayomi whispered.

Chenzira changed shoulders and continued trying to get his rest. "You are the worst. It is time to rest, and you do not sleep. You search for one who may not exist. You try to please an uncle who cannot be pleased. Abayomi, go to sleep."

"My mother is a beautiful woman. She is to be praised. She once served at the pharaoh's induction. The pharaoh asked for her personally," Abayomi said energetically.

"Truly, I have failed the gods because you will not be silent." Chenzira sat up and yawned. "You speak of your mother often. What of your father?"

Abayomi sulked slightly. He toiled with the sand beneath him. "I told you. He perished in the war. Chenzira, I'm afraid."

Chenzira sighed until he could create a suitable response. "It is okay to be afraid, Abayomi. Many times, being afraid has saved my life." Chenzira regained his supine posture and closed his eyes. "Besides, death cannot be that bad. You will see your father, once more." That was the extent of his concern for the boy.

Abayomi took no comfort in Chenzira's words. For the first time, he felt truly alone. When he was with his uncle, Abayomi could rely on Saabir's undeviating response. It was his one connection to Mosi. Alas, he believed Chenzira and knew his uncle was no more. *Even if I was still alive, would the crude farmer search for his missing nephew?* He had so many questions for his mother. *Why did you leave me? Why have you not come for me? Do you not love me?* These questions and many more laid the path to his slumber.

At dawn, Chenzira awoke to a long spear in front of his face. Holding that spear was a short, overweight man in a furry tunic and a skeletal mask shaped like a ram-like creature's skull. Chenzira assumed the man was Kushite by his complexion and the fact that he spoke in Meroitic. There twenty-or-so men like him there as well. One shoved Abayomi to consciousness. The boy rubbed his eyes to ensure he wasn't dreaming.

"Surrender to your foulness and almighty Seth, Egyptian follower," the man shouted.

^^^

Shabaka relished in the moment. The priests of Amon stood before the altar of the god of heavens and the dark skies above the Nile. The large, stone statue embodied the Hidden One, gold crown upon the pate and two giant ram horns protruding from his forehead. As the priests chanted, Shabaka, a large men of Kushite blood, knelt before the disciples of Amon. He stroked his bushy beard that hid the scar he suffered at the battle for Ashdod. Sargon was the better king on that day. However, Shabaka would let that wistfulness disappear for another day. On this day, he was accepting the honor of becoming the high priest of Memphis to accompany his living-god status. The pharaoh had embraced piety and dedicated his future to the gods and their whims. The chants ceased.

"It is without unwillingness that we accept what is before us and controls our very being," Shabaka said with cupped hands and closed eyes. "I choose to lead with an open heart, a passion to satisfy Great Amon, and to spread his word of omnipotence. This I swear to Egypt and very blood."

Further back in the shadows, a young Piye and Fadil knelt with many onlookers in the temple of jade and alabaster. They were coming-of-age at sixteen and six respectively. Both were small with their cotton tunics barely stable on their small frames. Beside them was their mother, a stunning, ebony beauty of regal ancestry. Her long braids appeared as though they were sculpted to conform to her striking cheeks and full lips. The entire city-state of Memphis attended the consecration, nearly thirty-thousand citizens.

"Will father forego battle to appease our new god?" Piye said to his mother.

"If Amon wills it, Piye," she whispered. "Your father will do what is required to protect Egypt and his family, as will you when the time comes."

Piye opened his eyes slightly to catch a glimpse of his brother. He placed a hand on Fadil's knee. "Fadil, I swear to keep you safe if I must. I swear it."

The young Fadil looked up at Piye and smiled. He did not comprehend the full extent of Piye's words, but he felt the warmth of his brother's sincerity.

Shabaka knelt humbly as the head priest placed the large plumes inside the back of Shabaka's tunic. Shabaka's leathery face hardened. His jaw tightened with each clench of his teeth. He pledged his very soul to the king of the gods.

"Mother, the feathers give father a harmonious guise," Piye whispered.

"Let us hope that harmony dissipates before your first battle to honor our land," she said without looking his direction. "Remember, a wise man will surely survive falling into a dark pit if he is accompanied by a proper fool. The priests are no friend to the pharaoh. Always remember that if you're ever fortunate to wield your father's power."

Piye nodded and closed his eyes in prayer.

Chapter Twelve

Piye awoke to the sounds of eagles cawing and the bright rays from Ra. His private chamber was airy that morning, due to the many attendants that opened every portal upon his awakening. They scurried around filling a variety of vessels and chamber pots. In his night clothes, a sleepy Piye scanned his surroundings. Once his vision came to focus, he saw Fadil sitting next to his bedding in his formal, embroidered tunic. He wore a wig of fine wool and leather sandals laced to his shins. Piye rose from his lying position.

"It is the Hour of the Rooster, my pharaoh," Fadil said softly. "Mother would like us to accompany her to The Many Blessings. You would have me wake you upon your insistence."

Piye espied the room frantically. "Boy, bring me wine!"

A diminutive attendant brought Piye a goblet of red wine. Piye raised the glass goblet above his head and drank the libation with complete fluidity. He wiped his course cheeks. "I was never fond of Tjenarian grapes, but they do not know any better." He faced Fadil. "I want to discuss the Assyrian threat."

"Do you think Sargon would challenge our might?" Fadil said with a perplexed look.

"Sargon is very much like his father, a man of little and unrealized consequence. We will face him eventually,"

Piye said as he stood. "Perhaps, I will take the battle to him." Piye sauntered over to his large wooden table where he displayed star charts and various hand drawn, geographical maps. After rustling for the map, he desired, he pointed to the colorless papyrus. "We will march to Sinai after first harvest. The grounds would give us a favorable advantage. We will have Re on our side. It is narrow as well."

Fadil was dumbfounded. Never had Piye consulted him on matters of war. He was relegated usually to trivial matters better suited for the city constable. Although he is the chief advisor and one of the best swordsmen in the lands, Piye had never confided in Fadil for battle tactics and strategies. Fadil met Piye at the map and nodded with an occasional groan.

"Would it not leave us at a disadvantage if our vanguard is overwhelmed? The Assyrians are formidable fighters, at the very least said by father," Fadil said.

Piye gazed at Fadil. "You will be my vanguard, brother. I believe such misfortune would not befall your aptitude for engagement."

"I see. I pray to Osiris that I am worthy," Fadil said with a slight bow.

"You are because I said you are," Piye replied stalwartly.

Fadil watched Piye tap a chime, signaling several manservants to enter his private chamber. They began dressing Piye in an arrangement of silk fabrics and ceremonial trinkets of sacred symbolism. Piye stood there dispassionately as the servants wrapped the robe with a cotton sash, allowing Piye to secure his khopesh on his waist. Piye took another sip of wine as they placed the final touch, a gold-hued, shoulder-length wig with his jeweled, bronze crown.

"Are you to dispense with government duties at this time?" Fadil said.

"I must tend to something much more tedious," Piye said with a sigh.

^^^

Chenzira and Abayomi were thrown at the feet of an elderly man. The robed man of modest appearance sat on a tree stump where a blazing campfire illuminated the entire encampment. He fondled his bushy beard and held tightly to a wooden staff. His eyes narrowed as he studied the young boys.

"I am Akil. You are among those who follow the true god. Whom do you serve?" the man said in Meroitic, a language Chenzira spoke scarcely.

The boys observed the camp nervously. Their hands being tied behind their backs with pig intestines caused this well-deserved emotion. Also, the hundred or so disheveled onlookers with ram-like skulls as masks and long spears contributed as well. Somehow, Chenzira managed to rise to his knees. Chenzira gave Abayomi a quick glance before focusing on Akil.

"We are simply citizens heading to the northern regions," Chenzira said.

"Whom do you serve?"

Chenzira hesitated before answering Akil, unsure of the correct response. Clearly, he assumed they were followers of Seth. However, uncertainty was a very formidable opponent. To say they were fellow followers might lead the two boys to a sacrificial conclusion, so he heard rumors in the alleys of Kerma. Although he did not worship any god, Chenzira felt it better to say otherwise.

"May Seth give you peace," Chenzira responded.

Akil stood and steadied himself with his staff. "Seth has given us the blessing of reason and character in his omnipotence. Even in his benevolence, he has granted his people the fortitude to hold what is true and the ability to foresee a lie." Akil gave the boys a sympathetic stare. "Sacrifice the non-believers."

Chenzira's eyes were wide open, and his jaw dropped with fright. "No, I speak the truth! We are Seth's children!"

The followers moved closer to the boys, aiming their spear tips downward. Revealing his limberness, Abayomi stammered to his feet. He took a deep breath and looked the high priest in the eyes directly. He was not afraid. He did not panic. He spoke in Meroitic calmly.

"Directed themselves by the Lake of the North, setting themselves towards the Mediterranean, which they desired to reach by sailing through the water district. But the god smote their hearts, and when they reached the middle of the waters as they fled, they directed themselves from the western lake to the waters which connect with the lakes of the district Mer, in order to join themselves there with the enemies who were the Land of Chaos."

The ancient writings stopped the followers in their tracks, leaving silence and the crackling of the campfire. Chenzira was in awe that such poetry was uttered by a farm boy barely out the womb. Akil gave Abayomi a sinister gaze before revealing a more amiable appearance. He smiled and motioned to nearby disciples to remove their bondage.

"We have young followers in our presence. We welcome Seth's children to worship in his glory. Untie them and share our meager provisions with our new members. It is fortuitous indeed."

Later that night, as most of the followers slept, Akil sat with Chenzira and Abayomi at the fire. A few of the followers accompanied them. They drank cups of hot ginger-root tea to warm their stomachs from the frigid, mountain breeze. Abayomi shivered after every sip, and the sheep skins they were given offered little comfort or warmth.

"It was not always this way," Akil said with a smile. "In Shabaka's reign, he cared for all the people of Egypt, particularly his kin. Piye has forgotten from whence he was born. He wishes to destroy our faction and praise one god only. He is without reason and humility."

Chenzira was thinking of the most advantageous escape from this old man's tribulations. He planned to make his escape when everyone slept. I'll leave Abayomi with them. Surely it would not be a burden for their way of life. Chenzira took another sip of the bitter drink, appreciating its warming properties.

"So, they want to find you. Why?" Akil said.

Chenzira wiped his wet mouth. "I am not sure. Perhaps, my father owes them a debt they hope I might pay. He was a degenerate, my father."

Akil nodded with sympathy. "Children cannot see the weight a father carries from a deep-rooted tree, but they only reason for existence. You should not blame him for his weakness. Most are without the blessing of Seth. May he give you peace."

"What of you? Why are you so far away from home?" Akil said in Abayomi's direction.

Abayomi lifted his head from between his knees. "I must reach Memphis. My mother waits for me there."

"Very far for such a small boy to travel, even with a friend," Akil said as he moved closer to the boy and took a knee. "My people are scattered. Piye has seen to that wickedness. Alas, we were forced from our homes, our families, and our land. So, we are traveling north to assemble with our brothers and take back what was taken from us. Stay with us, young Abayomi. We will take you to your mother."

Abayomi's eyes lit up. Akil's invitation was sent by the gods, perhaps from Seth. He wasn't sure. He cared only to see his mother again, though he could hardly distinguish her face from those years ago. "Yes, I will."

"Chenzira, will you stay with us as a child of the true god. We will protect you."

"I am tired. Can we rest and discuss it at dawn?" Chenzira said while yawning.

"I understand," Akil said as he flung the remaining tea from his cup. "To rest the body is to nourish one's soul. At dawn, we continue north and unify the believers."

Akil and the other beleaguered followers walked away from the campfire. Chenzira glanced at Abayomi and pondered whether he should leave the gullible child in these cult-like hands.

It didn't take long for everyone to fall sound asleep, including Abayomi. Chenzira and a couple guards posted by the followers were the exception. Chenzira rolled over to Abayomi and shook him profusely. Abayomi grimaced from having been awoken.

"Abayomi, wake up," Chenzira whispered as not to alert the guards.

"I want to sleep, Chenzira," Abayomi whispered back.

"Let us leave while we can escape," Chenzira pleaded.

"I will stay with them. They will take me to my mother."

"Do not trust these vagabonds. They wish only to bring you in their order. Let us go, now."

Abayomi thought for a split second and rested his head on the earth below. "No. I will stay. So should you."

100   "So be it," Chenzira said as slouched away. "You're a

foolish child."

Chenzira crept his way out of the encampment with no troubles, a skill he acquired long ago. He made his way through the thick brush, heading for the eastern bank of the Nile. He had gone a good distance before hearing the clangor of bronze weapons and the screams of fallen men. Upon gazing back at the Seth camp, he saw flames erupting from arrows soaring through the night sky and disappearing at the horizon.

"Son of Seth!" Chenzira began to move quickly down to the river. He then stopped, panting from adrenalin and fatigue. Chenzira faced the encampment again. Something pervaded his conscience, an emotion he had not experienced. The young Kushite was feeling empathy. He reconnected to the abandonment he felt as a child. He was compelled to go back for Abayomi.

"Foolish child," Chenzira muttered as he started back to the camp.

He reached the camp and found a hiding place in the thick brush on the outskirts of the Seth encampment. As he knelt and peeked through the long grasses, Chenzira saw the bronze, Egyptian leader saunter around with a torch in his hand. Fifteen remaining Seth disciples were hogtied and, on their knees, praying to their god. They were surrounded by the fallen, countless, bloody bodies. As Gahiji was speaking, he was setting one corpse at a time ablaze.

"I am a pragmatist," Gahiji said with a devilish smirk. "That is what my friends say is my most redeeming quality. Somehow, your leader escaped, but I could care less about an old fool. I want to know where the boy has gone. It is a simple question really." Another dead body erupts in flames. "You must understand, I do not care for your kind. You do not belong in my country. This is extremely important to me. Yet, I will have mercy for those who do not hinder my mission." Another dead body erupts in flames as the other musims observed with blood-stained khopeshes.

The smell was pungent as far as Chenzira nostrils. His eyes darted left and right in search of Abayomi. Perhaps, he escaped. Chenzira looked carefully, once more. He gazed upward into the trees and saw only smoke rising between the branches. After relinquishing hope to find the child, Chenzira turned to make his inconspicuous departure.

"Son of Seth," Chenzira said quietly. His heart was pounding.

Abayomi was kneeling behind him, a frightened boy who looked as if he lost his favorite toy. Abayomi placed his index finger over his lips. Chenzira gave him a look of a mixed cocktail of happiness and astonishment.

"How long were you behind me?" Chenzira said between gritted teeth.

Abayomi shrugged.

Chenzira glanced back at the encampment. He saw Gahiji looking their direction but did not see them. Chenzira took a deep swallow and dared not move. Gahiji appeared as though he was seeing through the brush and the entirety of Egypt. Gahiji squinted and returned to the desecration of the dead.

"We must go now," Chenzira said as he pushed Abayomi gently deeper into the dark brush.

^^^

Piye met his mother at her favorite gardens, private grounds she created during the time of Pharaoh Shabaka's reign. The garden was filled with every flora Egypt had to offer, daisies, water lilies, jasmine, roses, ivy, poppies, lotus, blackberries, and even more exceptionally exotic flowers. It was a bright, humid morning for them as they strolled through the heavily guarded sanctuary. Several handmaidens accompanied her. Five of Piye's personal bodyguards walked five feet behind him as well.

"The Seth order must be embraced in order to unify Egypt and secure our hold on the people, Piye," the queen mother said. "We will need their pious ways to resist any incursion by the Assyrians. Do not underestimate Sargon, Piye."

She wore a gold-hued dress of a silken fabric with embroidered jewels gleaming against the sunlight. Her braided wig was shoulder length and was highlighted with violet flowers from the southern coast of Hispania. Her face was decorated with heavy mascara and rouge.

"Embraced?" Piye said humorously. "I prefer to embrace them with my sword. They are a disease to Egypt and in need of being removed with a blade. They have made it clear that they will not be part of the greater good. They are vested in chaos and destruction. I will see to their demise, mother."

"Your father understood that the glory of a new Egypt 103

required that every citizen, from commoner to merchant, feel as though they were part of the land they built," the queen mother pleaded. "Piye, do you feel the gods gave you their power of life and death?"

"Yes," Piye said with his hands placed behind his back, a habit he often displayed when he felt righteous. "I am pharaoh, something you often forget, mother."

They both stopped and waved their escorts away, leaving them alone in the Garden of Tranquility. The queen mother and Piye held hands. She gave her son an expression of compassion and of resolve.

"Make peace with the Seth followers," the queen mother said. "However, this is what concerns me most. After we lost Theoris and the security of our bloodline, you and Bahiti must give Egypt an heir, yet you have barely spoken since that dreadful day."

"It matters not. I have an heir out there," Piye said as he let go of her hands. "I am a demon to Bahiti."

"Of course, there is the bastard. You would rather soil the purity of the family than lie with your queen and ensure our rule. I suppose Fadil could be better suited."

Piye returned his hands behind his back. "Oh, how has that gone, mother? Wives-to-be tend to not stay beside my brother for long."

"You must understand that Bahiti lost a child, a horror she has experienced far too many times. It may seem difficult at times, but you must keep trying for the land," the queen mother said with conviction.

"And I lost a son, again?" Piye hollered. "I believe in the prophecy. My son will rule beside me, with or without a mother."

Piye's mother caressed her son's forearm. "Go to her. She needs her pharaoh. She needs her brother."

"I must go, mother. It is good to see that you are well," Piye said as he walked away with his guards in tow.

Chapter Thirteen

Bahiti entered Rashidi's merkhet and saw the high priest gazing out the glass dome atop the cylindrical, stone structure. It towered nearly one hundred feet, and the observation sat atop the structure. Rashidi was using his astrolabe to examine the meteor shower, though categorized differently in that time. Rashidi ran his chubby fingers along the wood-carved astronomical instrument.

"My queen, look to Duat. Do you see what is happening? The gods are purging unworthy souls from their realm, the fallen, those who have gone astray from their commands," Rashidi said as continued to stare at the star-filled night sky.

Bahiti watched from over his shoulder. "It is beautiful. Death can be triumphant in the end," Bahiti said.

"I fear that the gods have grown angry with the pharaoh and are creating space for his early arrival," Rashidi said. "We must appease Osiris and his kingdom. A sacrifice would be appropriate."

"Did we not give the gods a generous offer ten moons ago?"

"Yes, my queen, but they were simple slaves, unworthy of a god's favor. We must offer more before the Nile rises upon the summer solstice," Rashid said as he turned to Bahiti. "Perhaps, a peasant child would suffice?"

Bahiti gave him a look of disgust. "I will not sacrifice another child for Piye's sake."

"As you wish, my queen," Rashidi said as he bowed and escorted Bahiti gently to a single torch on the chamber's northern wall, the only light source. Bahiti viewed hieroglyphs embedded in the wall. Some of it she could translate, however most of the ancient writings were indiscernible to her, due to the weathered stone of a thousand years.

Rashidi read the text for her. "A great cataclysm shall befall the people in the form of passion. Unyielding shall revenge fall upon thee. It is that we desire the most that will be the people's downfall. So speaks Osiris, the father and leader of us all. He who doubts the truth will fall to it."

"Why are you telling me this, Rashidi? Surely, you can cast a spell to protect us."

"My queen, I fear I cannot protect nor offer refuge from what is beyond my abilities. This dilemma dwells with the pharaoh and Duat." Rashidi stood before Bahiti. "Perhaps, the games will suffice, or our pharaoh must reconcile with what tortures him within."

∧∧∧

Chenzira and Abayomi arrived in Thebes in the middle of the night, the Hour of the Serpent. Chenzira knew of a hidden path that circumvented the city's high walls and the guards who stood upon them. They followed the main cobblestone road of the main square in bleak darkness. A torch on every corner of the avenue lit their path. Upon entering the walls of grandiose city-state, the boys were captivated by the stone Pillars of the Great Hypostyle Hall and the religious idolatry that pervaded the city. An occasional passerby walked by them on his or her way to a nearby establishment of social gathering and debauchery. Laughter danced in the air.

"We will take what we can and leave before morning," Chenzira said as he espied his surroundings. "Those men cannot be far behind."

Abayomi rubbed his belly. "Are you not starved?"

Chenzira looked flabbergasted. "Hungry? I am happy to be alive. Besides, Hunger requires food, and food requires currency. That is something we don't possess. We will gather food in the hills."

Abayomi reached in the crotch of his loincloth and withdrew a pouch. He attempted to hand it to Chenzira, but he refused to take it. Abayomi shook it, creating the rattle of coins.

"What is that?" Chenzira said, perplexed.

"I have been saving here and there for when I would travel to my mother," Abayomi said as he exposed the pouch's contents. It was filled with several bronze coins, enough for two meals and more.

Chenzira rubbed his narrow chin. "I suppose we can have repast here, but we must leave as soon as possible."

"Yes," Abayomi concurred as he nodded.

"What should we do?" Chenzira said gleefully.

"I stink of fish. I want a warm bath," Abayomi said as he sniffed his tunic. "I want a real bath, no river bath. I want a warm bath."

Chenzira rubbed his chin. "I know of a place in Thebes that a friend of mine once told me about. He said they gave great baths."

Chenzira found the storefront sign from his recollection. The immaculate, white structure had an old-world appeal with latticed windows and a balustrade veranda overlooking the stone-paved road below. Outside the entrance, there was a limestone statue of a nude, pleasing woman. Chenzira knocked on the door. They could hear footsteps on the other side, and a lady's face appeared in a small, sliding window.

"We are closed," the woman said. "All the girls have gone to sleep."

Both boys shrugged; obviously, unaware they have stumbled upon a brothel. Chenzira showed the pouch of coins. He jingled it to reveal its contents.

"We wish to have a bath, madam," Chenzira said. "We can pay."

It wasn't long before several latches were disarmed, and the door opened. An older woman stood before them with long hair and a pale face of exotic origin. She didn't appear Egyptian to Chenzira.

"Welcome, young warriors," the slender woman said. "I am Nilwana, proprietor."

The boys entered the establishment and was taken immediately to a dimly lit sitting room with exquisite chandeliers, a large round table that allowed for dining on the carpeted floor, and paintings depicting the carnal inclinations of men and women, the latter giving the boys pause. They met Nilwana's older sister and soon were eating rare delicacies from across the sea, shellfish, reptiles, and the unidentifiable. They washed everything down with red wine. Very quickly, they both were inebriated as Nilwana sat with them to ensure their goblets remained full.

"I will find my mother," Abayomi said, after gulping down another mouthful of the sweet nectar.

"That is very brave for such a young boy," Nilwana said with a smile. "To travel alone takes great courage."

"I am not alone. I have Chenzira. He is my brother."

Chenzira shook his head. "I think the wine has caused his mind to betray him."

Nilwana laughed. "I have seen much younger boys overcome their rite of passage. Besides, he reminds me of someone from my past. What is your mother's name? If I see her, I will tell her that her handsome boy searches for her."

"Her name is Mosi, and you will never see her because she is in Memphis," Abayomi said with a hint of sarcasm.

Nilwana's face stiffened. "Mosi, you say? She is of Kush, the same as you?"

Abayomi nodded. Chenzira was bewildered. Nilwana's

eyes lit up, and she looked Abayomi in his eyes.

"She is small," Nilwana said as she squinted. "Yes, I see it. You are the son she told me about. I know your mother."

"You know her," Abayomi said in astonishment. "How do you know her?"

Nilwana seemed to awake from a trance. "That is inconsequential. I know where you can find her. She is not in Memphis. I will take you to her at dawn."

Chenzira appeared unconvinced. In his opinion, it was too serendipitous for such fortune too befall the young Kushite, almost prophetic. He never trusted anyone, regardless of their amiability. However, he cared about Abayomi and feared the young, gullible child would be lost without him. "If you knew of Abayomi, why had you not gone to him?" Chenzira said after taking another sip.

"Your mother wanted your protection. Mosi planned to hide you away with your uncle until it was safe," Nilwana said and stood. "I swore to her that I would keep her secret, and she would notify me when the time was most auspicious. Where is your uncle?"

"I fled," Abayomi replied. "Safe from what?"

"It is late. I will explain at dawn, young Abayomi. Rest after your bath." Nilwana departed.

Two hours later, the boys were frolicking and soaking their night away at the bathhouse portion of the brothel. The pool was empty, except for Nilwana and her sister, who began prepping the place for the next day, replacing the candles and such. They sat there naked in the warm pool of water with their bellies full and smiles on their faces. They were surrounded by opaque limestone and statues serving as fountains. The trickling of water calmed them both, even for just a moment.

"The bath was a good idea, Chenzira," Abayomi said with his eyes closed. He looped his fingers through the pleasant steam bath.

"It is," Chenzira replied. "We are missing fruit to help us embrace this moment. I have not had a warm bath since..." Chenzira searched his thoughts for a couple seconds. "I have not bathed properly since I got away."

"Where did you escape from, from whom?" Abayomi was intrigued. He did not truly know much about Chenzira's past. He only knew that the young man was distant at times.

Chenzira was silent. He stared at Abayomi in awe of his innocence and in resentment of his naivety. He could not bring himself to recall those days. Pain became his closest friend, and perseverance was a nearby illusion that came to his rescue.

"Do you trust her, Abayomi?"

"Yes," Abayomi said without hesitation.

"I guess it is time to part ways. I'll find one of the ladies to give us the fruit we need," Chenzira said as his wiry frame exited the pool.

Abayomi shook his head as Chenzira darted away. He practiced holding his breath under water, the way Chenzira taught him. He came above water seconds later, coughing and choking. He didn't have to relieve himself.

^^^

Piye entered his throne room with Rashidi and a squad of his finest personal guards. He wore his Blue Crow for the gathering, a kepresh he traditionally wore when leading men in battle. In addition to his leather sandals and tunic, he was dressed in his ceremonial cloak with bronze pieces, a symbol of his dominion over the people of Egypt. He sat in his throne and Rashidi stood behind him.

"Shall we?" Piye said, clenching the armrests.

The robed high priests of their respective deity sat on pillows in a semi-circle before him. From left to right sat the high priests of the Horus, Re, Ptah, Anubis, Hathor, Bastet, Thoth, and Amon factions. The only female representative was Ralia, the high priestess of Isis, a middle-aged woman of petite stature. She was a woman that Piye respected. Ralia served his father during the warring years. Piye had known her to be stubborn but fair. She had her convictions but was practical, nonetheless.

"My pharaoh, Akil was once a member of this council, yet he is no longer welcome. The Seth high priest is still a servant of Duat," Ralia said in her youthful tone. "He served your father very well, and his followers desire your greater glory."

"Is that so?" Piye said jokingly. "Perhaps, their god has not told them this much. They riot in my cities and make 113 claims of righteousness that surpasses even me. The land would be better off without them. Besides, we have so many gods. What is one less?"

Rashidi chuckled until he saw the disenchanted stares from his colleagues on the floor. Ralia had that way of intimidation without uttering a single word. The Egyptian priestess had eyes that were piercing as well as enchanting.

"That might be true, my pharaoh. However, a member of the Seth sect has routinely been present for all spiritual advisory meetings," Ralia said sternly. "On this day, he and his flock have been scattered in fear of retribution from you."

"The pitiful nihilists are hiding in Nuri! I will root them out and erase them from Egyptian memory!" Piye said as his chest heaved up and down.

"I must ask, we must ask, why does the pharaoh harbor such hatred for these people?" Ralia said. "What message are you sending to the rest? Every spiteful god is condemned to oblivion, so spoken by Osiris. Are they not?"

Rashidi cleared his throat. "High priestess, which is interpreted by the ancient writings, far removed from any modern logic." He gave Piye a look for approval.

"Let us forego this petty chatter, my pharaoh. We demand that you let the Seth sect back into the fold," Ralia said without mincing words. "There will be no more capture, murder, or expulsion of their followers. Even you must answer to the gods, Pharaoh."

The other priests, including Rashidi, turned away in astonishment to her austerity. Piye sat on the edge of his throne. He placed his hands to his lips as though praying. There was an uncomfortable silence, except for the flicker of torched illuminating the chamber.

"Ah, I must answer to myself," Piye said as he nodded. "Is that so? It seems I am at a peculiar junction. Since I am a living god, I do not have to answer to anyone on this plane of existence."

Ralia was unyielding. She knew that Isis was her sole salvation and ruler of the afterlife. She did not fear death. She did not fear Piye.

"It is that way of surmising that viewpoint that led to the destruction of previous rulers, my pharaoh," Ralia stated. "You would be wise not to upset the gods, all of them."

Piye chuckled. "High Priestess Ralia, I will not upset the natural order of things. From this point, I will no longer succumb to the personal removal of the Seth. Would that be satisfactory to this council?"

The priest nodded in unison as Piye, and his entourage, stormed out of the chamber. The priests bowed their heads to the floor to the heavy footsteps. Ralia lifted her head and remained unmoved.

^^^

Abayomi began getting restless. He wondered what was delaying Chenzira. Also, he noticed he had not seen a bath-house servant in some time. Abayomi was alone. He grew impatient and exited the pool. His loincloth was soaked, 115 and he was dripping water. He shivered from a slight breeze. Breath vapor spewed from his mouth and nose. As he made his way from the bath area into the next room, his eyes darted from left to right. He pushed the bamboo door open. It creaked open. Before he could scream, a hand from nowhere covered his mouth.

Chenzira had a khopesh to his throat and was surrounded by several musims. Gahiji stepped from behind his henchmen, displaying a smile of satisfaction. The women who operated the place were dismembered flesh. Nilwana's eyes were still open though she was not breathing. Blood soaked the tiled flooring. Abayomi let out a horrific scream.

Gahiji took a knee before the boy. His face contorted to a more serious demeanor. "You boys are very resourceful, but now, I have you."

^^^

Fadil decided to show Catena his collection of rare animals he had acquired throughout the Serengeti. Various cages housed an assortment of wild beasts, from a Katanga lion to a bonobo ape. This zoological garden was located just inside the walls surrounding Napata. Piye allowed his brother such idiosyncrasies. The moon was full, and torches lit their way. The two walked arm in arm.

Fadil was dressed in his finest military dress wear. He wore a white satin tunic with the pharaoh's crest embroidered into the delicate fabric. His sandals were laced with bronze straps, and he displayed a few trinkets around his neck. A metallic headband separated his handsome face from his cropped hair. He hunched slightly to compensate for his obvious height difference over the dark-haired beauty. Catena was wearing a colorful, long, A-line cotton skirt and an onionskin shawl. Her hair draped down her back, and her face reminded Fadil of a finely polished jewel, free from impurities.

"I am more attracted to the cats. I have been since I was a child," Fadil said while blushing.

Catena walked over to the lion's cage. She knelt as the stealthy creature greeted her at the bars. Fadil was stunned as Catena extended her hand between the bars and rubbed its mane, ever so gently. Fadil was left speechless with her early familiarity.

"Cats are predatory creatures, yet they have a gentle nature about them," Catena said with a smile. "In Messana, we believe they can see a man's soul. That is why they fear us, though they would easily slay us to defend their young, their brood. Do you agree?"

Fadil took a moment to gather his thoughts. "I believe putting your hand in that cage is not a wise decision."

Catena chuckled. "Why? He has searched my soul and knows that I mean him no harm."

"You are far too trusting."

"Am I," Catena said as she stood and held Fadil's hands. "It is easy to trust something when you do not fear it."

"That is…," Fadil started to say and contemplated his response. "That was said by someone who doesn't live beside lions. Do you agree?"

117

They continued their stroll. The hook-lipped rhinoceros stopped Catena in her tracks. She watched as the thick-skinned, black, powerful mammal chewed a thorny bush provided by the caretakers. She wondered if the cage would hold it if it became annoyed.

"I fear I will have to leave this land. My father warns of a war brewing from the east," Catena said.

"Is that so?" Fadil said, pretending to be ignorant of the Assyrians. "Not to worry, my brother is a strong leader. He will ensure Egypt's victory."

Catena walked past him. "Now, who is far too trusting?"

Fadil caught up to her. "Regardless, we are prepared. I train my men rigorously at each dawn."

"That must make you very popular."

Fadil held her hands. "I do not need many friends, only a few."

^^^

Bahiti gazed out the window of her private chamber that overlooked the courtyard of the Pyramid of Great Gatherings. It was an elegant accommodation with flora and candles throughout the spacious room. Statues of Isis covered the limestone walls and numerous texts sat atop luxurious jade furnishings. It was the boudoir of the queen, one level below the pharaoh's.

A soldier that normally stood guard outside her door entered. "My queen, he is here."

"Let him enter." Bahiti ensured her evening dressing gown was secure.

A diminutive man of Egyptian ancestry entered with his eyes on the floor. He prostrated himself immediately. He wore a grungy robe, and his sandal-clad feet appeared to be soiled. "My queen, forgive me for my appearance. I never expected to have an audience with a goddess."

Bahiti waved the guard away, and the door closed behind him. Bahiti approached the peasant. She gazed down at him and had a very stoic, yet typical, expression. The man was much older than the queen, however they did not dwell on the same plane of existence.

"You may rise," Bahiti said softly.

The man rose slowly to his feet while staring at the floor. He never dared looking at her directly. It could have cost him more than just his eyes.

"You are the best artisan in Napata, I understand," she said.

"Yes, Great Royal Wife. My work is shown throughout the kingdom as well as Phoenicia. What is your bidding?"

"Can you replicate another piece?"

"Great Royal Wife, I can create what is necessary as you command."

"That is pleasing."

Chapter Fourteen

The day of the chariot races brought commoners, courtiers, and foreign dignitaries to the enormous coliseum that's centered in Napata. It was a grand outdoor arena, circular as anyone would expect. Its stone rows seated nearly ten thousand spectators, and statues of Osiris towered above everyone. The tantara announced the first race was beginning. It was an especially dry and blistering afternoon. Piye, Fadil, Bahiti, Rashidi, the head priests, and several Egyptian guards took umbrage on his royal balcony, overlooking the dirt track. Piye was wearing his ceremonial coiffure, a tunic bottom, and a gold medallion, given to him by his father many moons ago. As the crowd cheered below, Piye approached the edge of the balustrade veranda and stared down at the thousands he considered his children. He raised a palm to settle the roar that came from his appearance.

"Let me be forthwith with my introduction on this day!" Piye said as his voice carried well in the giant space. "The days of arrogating Egypt are no longer. We are prosperous, void of tragic misfortune that had plagued our people for far too long. We are one people, one Egypt, and soon, one god."

The self-effacing priests looked to one another in disbelief. Ralia, the high priestess of Isis, gave the pharaoh an inconspicuous scowl. Bahiti was expressionless as though she was not present.

"What is Egypt? It is the people! The pious drolls would

have you believe differently. What is Egypt if not for the people, the Egyptians and the Kushites together, one? There are those who are lost in the past. They want to rip Egypt from the annals of mankind. That is why I will fight and die to realize the dream of my father, of Shabaka, Egypt's greatest pharaoh. For he knew, for Egypt to flourish, we will as one. Let these races announce a dream fulfilled!"

There was a melodic applause that followed.

"SON OF RE!"

"SON OF RE!"

"SON OF RE!"

As Piye waved, Ralia leaned forward and whispered into Rashidi's ear, "Such specious reasoning will lead to our downfall. We must remind him of his impieties."

Rashidi had a look of concern but brushed her off as one does a fly. In the end, he knew he represented the "one god" Piye referenced. He was quite adroit when it came to securing his wellbeing.

The chariots began filling the arena in parade form. Each competitor, a rugged collection of former slaves and battle-tested warriors, bowed as their chariots passed Piye, giving tribute to their living god. They held tightly to their reins to move their steeds to the starting line. They wore a variety of armor, some plate, some chain, and some leather. Their weaponry varied as well, spears, swords, halberds, maces, and a few with bows and arrows. There was a total of fifteen in the first race. The main objective was to finish   121 the race alive. The length was three complete laps around the inner circumference of the coliseum. As the horses danced around neighing with nostrils aquiver, Piye raised a single, open hand. To create higher anticipation, he waited for a moment and made a fist. The race had begun.

As the competitors made their way around the track, they each took the opportunity to eliminate a speedier horse and chariot. Controlled chaos ensued. The heavy hooves and solid wheels lifted a cloud of dust and debris in their wake. The clangor of arms permeated the track. Swords clashed and spears found their mark. Crimson blood splattered as men fell to their death. An occasional limb flew as if it was a prelude to a horrific scream. A field of fifteen dwindled to eight by the first lap. One competitor in particular fell from his chariot and fell prey to the real power of the horse-drawn war chariots. His body parts were quickly separated as though he was never a man at all. Piye and the crowd enjoyed the mayhem.

"That looked painful," Piye said from his seat, laughing.

"It is barbaric for men to die without battle and the promise of an honorable death," Fadil said with a look of disgust. "They will never enter the kingdom of Osiris."

"You need not fret, Fadil. I have blessed these men with the wishes of a pharaoh."

Fadil glanced at Bahiti. He noticed that she was silent and in deep thought. Ever since Theoris' death, he grew concerned for her health. They never had the chance to speak on the death of his nephew.

"So, tell me of this Etruscan woman you have met," Piye said while keeping his eyes on the race. "Do not be surprised, brother. I see all. I do have the Eye of Horus."

Fadil was surprised initially, and then he remembered his brother's need to pry. "I met her at the market. She is an importer of foreign goods."

Piye faced Fadil with a look of chagrin. "Her father is a merchant of foreign goods. He is a simple parvenu of little importance. Rid yourself of her. I have someone else in mind for you. I do not want our bloodline contaminated with that of a foreigner."

Fadil's first instinct was to defend Catena's honor and his manhood. However, he feared his brother, and he knew the ramifications of quarreling with him. Therefore, he did what he had typically done. Fadil nodded and pretended to watch the blood sport beneath him.

Piye looked to his left and was taken aback by Bahiti staring intensely at the pharaoh. It wasn't a look of pure anger. It was the stare one does when they witness the very moment the sun disappears below the horizon, the moment darkness was taking hold and the fears that accompanied it. Piye gave an uncomfortable smile to his wife and returned his attention to the race.

^^^

Osiris stepped into the sandstorm. The king was bandaged, and blood smeared his face. The land was barren, and floods raged from sky to earth. The desert was volcanic, and the sky rained brimstone. Lightning illuminated mounds of deceased souls. It was a land of chaos. It was 123 *the land of Seth.*

Osiris approached his carnivorous sibling, who sat on a throne constructed of skeletal remains and ashes. Seth waved his tale as his brother approached, amazed that Osiris still existed. He held tight to the hilt of his giant battle-axe. They were alone. Osiris was unarmed.

"Your betrayal is contemptible and must be rebutted," Osiris said in a resonant tone. "Alas, you will suffer your demise, Seth."

Seth rose with his battle-axe in both paws. "It is you, brother, who will suffer his demise, for you are unarmed."

"You seek destruction and power at any cost. You have lied, cheated, and chosen to deny the very birthright that enables your arrogance. You wish to strike me down. If that is your wish, so be it. However, I have something you will never possess, something you will never contort to your ugly ambitions. Isis has given me a son. You tell me I am without the ability to defend myself? I possess a sword you will never have in your clutches. I have the truth."

Suddenly, Horus appeared behind Seth. He was the very essence of mystical beauty. Horus was muscular and had a long, flowing mane. He appeared as though he was sculpted from jade, not of human flesh. He embodied the exquisiteness of his mother, in male form. Horus placed a hand on Seth's torso, causing Seth to fall immediately to his hind legs. His skin began disintegrating into dust. Seth swung his giant battle-axe and sliced the left eye of Horus, removing the eyeball all together.

124   *Horus cried out in agony as Osiris moved in for the kill.*

Seth regained his feet and awaited his melee with his brother. Osiris reached his throat before Seth could react. Seth gasped and raised his weapon.

"Cease your bickering!" Isis said as she materialized behind her husband.

She grabbed Osiris by the forearm. "Yes, we must learn truth. We must learn forgiveness as well. Let us be of one purpose."

As Osiris calmed down slowly from his rage, he released Seth. "You are right, my wife. I have forgotten our way. I swear to you, brother, we will wage war no longer. This you must swear to me and your brother's son. Do you be of the same mind?"

Seth nodded.

"It is settled. We will live in peace for all of eternity," Isis said joyfully.

Seth nodded once more. His amiable smile was truly deceptive, for he could not purge himself of the jealousy, bitterness, and hatred he felt for Osiris. So, he hid his snarl. He bowed graciously. He spoke in propitious fashion. Yet, he decided he would wait and exact his revenge.

^^^

Fadil was stroking his African wildcat, Sheba, as darkness began to fill his private chamber. The torches provided ample light, though he grew weary of reviewing the ancient volumes of triumphs by Ramses the Second. So, he sat there abed in faint lighting, contemplating Piye's words of 125 shunning Catena. There were moments he understood. *Piye desires what is best for me, for our family. Alas, his very punctilious nature keeps him two steps ahead.*

Fadil heard two knocks before the door crept slowly open. The hooded figure visited Fadil, once again. He entered and closed the chamber's door behind him. The shadowy, silhouette of a man stood there, motionless. Sheba meowed, leaped from Fadil's lap, and disappeared into the darkness.

"His impatience is teetering on rage, chief advisor," The dark figure whispered. "You swore to eliminate him, did you not?"

"I promised him the keys to Egypt, not my brother's blood," Fadil said as he stood. "I will not be manipulated any further. You tell him that my work is complete. I will not betray my brother's life!"

"I will convey your message to my liege. Are you breaking your promise, chief advisor?"

Fadil nodded hesitantly.

With that, the mysterious emissary exited the room, leaving Fadil alone with thoughts of regret.

^^^

Piye rode Kawa through the grassy plain. The sky was bright and colorless. A fog enveloped the ground. Kawa jumped a considerable obstacle of withered skeletons. Piye was pleased. A lone figure appeared before him. Kawa trot-
126 *ted forward to give Piye a closer glimpse of the ghostly*

spirit. He could not distinguish or categorize the apparition.

"What do you want?" Piye shouted from his saddle.

Its head tilted to the side, and its arms were extended, reaching for the opportunity to take hold of the pharaoh. Piye drew his khopesh as Kawa neighed and his nostrils quivered. Piye held tightly to the reins. Suddenly, the figure raced towards him, gliding above the earth.

Piye could not steady his stallion. He could not put himself in position to defend himself. The figure was upon him.

"You must know repentance!" the figure shrieked.

Piye was overcome with fear. Cold streamed through his veins. He knew death was upon him.

Chapter Fifteen

Gahiji had the boys chained and led them to their encampment on the outskirts of Thebes. Abayomi and Chenzira were flung to the sand provided by the clearing. The mountain air was crisp and bitter from an occasional night breeze. A large cart that was requisitioned by the musims arrived at camp. It still had remnants of straw inside. The horse that pulled it was feasible at best. Thirty of the musims assembled at the camp.

"I will take the boy with me in the wagon," Gahiji said as he transferred his paraphernalia from his chariot to the cart. "Bring my chariot along."

Chenzira struggled with his hands chained behind his back. "Let the boy go. Why do you hold him hostage as well?"

Gahiji paused for a moment before approaching Chenzira. "Is that what you think he is, or you?"

Gahiji gave a sinister smirk and sat beneath a tree. "We will camp for the night and leave at dawn. Send a message to the rest. Also, notify the pharaoh. His blood is not to be taken when Re is not present. It is written in the prophecy."

The musims did as charged as Gahiji rested his head against the tree trunk. He closed his eyes and placed his khopesh on his lap. He began his prayer, and the moon was full and ominous.

"Glory be to thee, Osiris Un-nefer, the great god who dwellest within Abtu, thou king of eternity, thou lord of everlastingness, who passest through millions of years during thine existence. Thou art the eldest son of the womb of Nut, and thou wast engendered by Seb, the Ancestor; thou art the lord of the crowns of the South and North, thou art the lord of the lofty white crown, and as prince of gods and men thou hast received the crook, and the whip, and the dignity of his divine fathers. Let thine heart, O Osiris, who art in the Mountain of Amentet, be content, for thy son Horus is stablished upon thy throne. Thou art crowned lord of Tettu, and ruler in Abtu. Through thee the world waxeth green in triumph before the might of Neb-er-tcher. He leadeth in his train that which is, and that which is not yet, in his name Ta-her-sta-nef; he toweth along the earth by Maat in his name of Seker; he is exceedingly mighty and most terrible in his name Osiris; he endureth forever and forever in his name of 'Un-nefer. Homage is to thee, O King of kings, Lord of lords, Ruler of princes, who from the womb of Nut hast ruled the world and the Underworld. Thy members are like bright and shining copper, thy head is blue like lapis-lazuli, and he greenness of the turquoise is on both sides of thee, O thou god an of millions of years, whose form and whose beauty of face are all-pervading in Ta-tchesert. He will lead us."

As the evening progressed, Chenzira and Abayomi were hogtied near the campfire. They both were on their stomachs, fighting the hold of their chains. Two musims stood guard along the perimeter while Gahiji and the rest were fast asleep.

"Chenzira, I am afraid. I do not want to die," Abayomi said as tears rolled down his cheeks.

"Abayomi, we will escape this madness," Chenzira whispered. "Have I ever failed you?"

Abayomi shook his head.

"You will see your mother again," Chenzira said with a determined glare.

Chenzira and Abayomi did not sleep the entire night. At sunrise, they were groggy and weary from the long night. Gahiji washed his hands and face in a pail provided by one of his henchmen. His bronze, leathery skin was cleansed of the filth from the past month. He dabbed his cobra tattoo with a dry cloth. As the musims prepared to abandon camp, Gahiji approached the two boys. He removed a key from his waist and unchained Chenzira. The wiry teen stood awkwardly, carefully finding his balance. Abayomi shivered on the ground.

"You have me now! You can let the boy go," Chenzira pleaded.

Gahiji placed a hand on Chenzira's shoulder. "I knew one day you would lead us. The prophecy was correct as predicted by the pharaoh. You are the light that guides the eagle through darkness. It is fitting a new day begins here on this mountain."

Chenzira appeared bewildered. He did not understand the words uttered by Gahiji. He thought to sprint away, but he decided against it. He was weak, and he did not want to leave Abayomi. He would rely on punctilious vernacular to save Abayomi's life.

"He is just a child. You will be cast to the underworld

to suffer agony for eternity," Chenzira said as a single tear streamed down his face. "I am here to pay what my father has owed. Search the goodness that lives in every man's heart."

Gahiji gazed at Chenzira. His eyes were void of compassion or anger. He looked at Abayomi for a moment and returned his focus to Chenzira.

"I knew one day you would be the one who would lead us... to him," Gahiji said as he gestured towards Abayomi.

Before Chenzira could react, Gahiji unsheathed his khopesh and ran the boy through and through. Chenzira's entrails dripped from the tip of Gahiji's blade. Chenzira's mouth was wide open, and blood trickled from his nose and other orifices. He could not scream. Chenzira had a look of disbelief as his limp body fell to the ground, perishing instantly. Abayomi buried his face in the dirt, bellowing from the sudden horror of witnessing the death of his protector.

Gahiji wiped his blade with his washcloth. "Put the boy on the cart. We have a three-day journey ahead of us."

A couple of musims loaded Abayomi on the horse-drawn cart as though he was unsuspecting cattle.

^^^

Piye was brushing a mare as Bahiti walked into the pharaoh's personal stable, ground level of the Pyramid of Great Gatherings. The horse barn housed several of Piye's prized horses, including Kawa. He made it his purpose to visit his greatest joys in life, frequently. Bahiti was accompanied by two ladies-in-waiting until she dismissed them to be alone with her husband. The Great Royal Wife stood behind Piye as he brushed intensely. She had a look of disgust from the odor emanating from animal sweat and dung.

"The treasurer worries that the expenditure for the pyramid in Theoris's name delays necessary dam repairs," Bahiti said. "He was adamant about the threat of flooding."

"There has not been a flood of the Nile in two generations," Piye said while he continued to brush. "He can never have enough slaves. His specious reasoning is why he chirps to a woman instead of discussing the matter at the council meetings."

Bahiti chuckled. "Perhaps, you are correct. Regardless, I told him I would bring the matter to you myself."

"That is most propitious of you, sister," Piye said with a smile and continued the task at hand. "Why are you here?"

"Tell me, Piye, do you think Theoris was taken from us for our past transgressions?"

Piye stopped brushing and glared at Bahiti. "Your mercurial temperament can be very trying at times, Bahiti."

Just as Piye responded, a member of his personal guard rushed in and handed Piye a scroll. He bowed, and Piye waved him away. Piye read the papyrus and smiled profusely.

"He found him." Piye was ecstatic as he looked at Bahiti. "The prophecy came true."

"Congratulations, Piye," Bahiti said. "You now have your bastard."

"Do you not understand?" Piye pleaded. "I now have an heir. We have an heir. Egypt has an heir. Our family will rule for ten thousand moons."

"Something was born from your seed," Bahiti said with a look of chagrin. "Alas, our union can be the only culprit. Do you even remember, Theoris? You are a pretender."

Piye tossed the brush and held Bahiti's hands. "Am I to blame that my consorts give me daughters? You are free from blame, my wife. Your womb is putrid, a hostile environment. How many children have we lost? Two? Three? The gods have decided to free you of the burden. Be joyous."

Instantly, Bahiti slapped Piye in anger. Piye lurched backward and wiped the blood that trickled from his bottom lip. He glanced at his hand to confirm his injury. Rage overcame him, and he sprung in her direction for their long-awaited fight. Piye reached for her throat to no avail. Bahiti was trained in the martial arts and evaded his grasp easily, allowing Piye's weight to carry him to the dirt. His long, salt-and-pepper hair was disheveled, and his tunic was soiled.

"Son of Seth, you asked for this," Piye said as he clenched his teeth.

Piye swung with a heavy fist. Bahiti caught it, and soon Piye found his arm restrained behind has back. Bahiti kissed him on the neck.

"You are slowing with age, brother," Bahiti whispered in his ear.

The warrior within kicked in. Piye tilted his head back and headbutted Bahiti. She fell on her bottom. Quickly, she regained her footing and began a series of frontal kicks, narrowly missing Piye's head. Piye, blocked the last kick attempt and followed with a punch to Bahiti's belly. She fell like a dying tulip, gasping and coughing from lack of air.

"Enough!" Piye said as his chest pounded from adrenalin. "I should have you crucified."

"Every sunrise, I pray that you would."

Piye looked at his sister and wife with a moment of sadness. "Why do you hurt me? How did you become such a bitter soul? I think about Theoris with every breath I take!"

The ladies-in-waiting rushed in to help their queen off the ground. Bahiti stood and glared at Piye with a look that could cut stone. She adjusted her cotton tunic and decorative wig.

"The queen is not well. Escort her to her chamber," Piye said in an exhausted tone.

Chapter Sixteen

Gahiji appropriated a trireme at Aswan to sail back to Napata on the Nile. It was a massive military vessel with three rows of oars and a battering ram at its prow. The ship belonged to the pharaoh's navy and had a crew of twenty seamen and a complement of slave rowers. It was near dusk, and they were passing Kerma when the skies opened. Rain pummeled the deck. Gahiji and Abayomi sat in the captain's quarters. Abayomi sat in the corner of the nondescript room, except for the occasional nautical map. His hands were still restrained behind his back.

"Are you hungry?" Gahiji said nonchalantly.

Abayomi nodded, and Gahiji released the boy from bondage. Abayomi rubbed his wrists to restore circulation. Gahiji tossed a sliver of dried meat at Abayomi. Like a wild dog, Abayomi began devouring the salty lamb chunk.

"You are son of a pharaoh. You will know unimaginable power, Abayomi."

"He is not my father! My father died!"

Gahiji crouched before Abayomi. "Really? What does your father look like? What is his name? How did he die? You know nothing about your father because the pharaoh is your blood."

Abayomi gave him a forbidding glare. "I know how you will die. You will pay for killing my friend."

Gahiji stood up and laughed. "Get in line, Kushite. I have killed many friends."

"Do you know where my mother is?" Abayomi said.

"No," Gahiji answered as the boat rocked from side to side. "You can ask your father in due time."

"Chenzira had a good heart. Why did you have to kill him? It was me you were searching for all along." Abayomi threw the remaining meat to the floor and sobbed.

"For the prophecy to become reality, he had to die. That was the cost for you, a soul for another. Do not cry. He will be honored in Duat. He has served Osiris's purpose. One day, you will be pharaoh, and I will serve you as I serve your father. Upon that day, you will know the price for power."

"The only thing you will serve are the dogs at Seth's feet," Abayomi said.

Gahiji sat on a nearby crate. He pulled out a sliver of dry lamb meat and started chewing on the rubbery morsel. His eyes became slits, and he grinned, not from joy but from cynicism.

"It would please me to die, once more."

^^^

"Mother, must we discuss it now?" Piye said while turning his back on the queen mother. "This is a great day."

136   The Temple of Osiris was constructed by Piye's order.

Limestone blocks were layered in a cubic, pyramid fashion. The entire structure was coated in white ivory, which gave the temple of worship a surreal appearance under the sunlight. At its apex stood a menacing, alabaster statue of Osiris and Isis, holding baby Horus from their thrones, ruling over their earthly minions. Inside the religious refuge were stone pillars and the stories of Egyptian floods and seasonal crop abundance carved in its walls. The spacious hall was well lit by cascading sunbeams. Several lower priests were going about their day to the harmonious chanting emanating from the main prayer chamber. Piye and his mother approached the statue of his father, Shabaka the Uniter. The queen mother lit a candle in her husband's memory. She wore a black robe, customary for a widow to wear on Remembrance Day. They both prayed at the feet of the departed warrior king while a contingent of Piye's personal guards lined the walls.

"It is said that Akil is afraid to show himself for fear of retribution," she said. "He fears for his people. The followers of Seth were here long before Egypt was conceived."

"Father always said he was a wise man," Piye replied with a sarcastic smile.

"If you decide to war with Sargon, we will need him and his followers. You would be wise to listen to those who have seen more than you could ever fathom."

Piye faced her. "You are my mother, and you are a fountain of wisdom. However, I am pharaoh. This building you are praying within was built by me. Napata was built by me. Prosperity has reigned from Khartoum to the Nile Delta because of me. I am guided by Osiris. He possesses the only wisdom I need."

The queen mother folded her arms, closed her eyes, and nodded. She raised her index finger and took a deep breath. She then placed her hand on his chest.

"Piankhy, how did I lose you? You were once a very happy child. Now, you have become a heartless man."

Piye was surprised that she used his childhood name. It was reserved before for administering punishment when he was a lad. He smiled and hugged her.

"Your eyes take you places your mind cannot see," Piye said in a playful tone. "Cease your worry, mother. I am a benevolent pharaoh."

She opened her eyes and caressed his hands. "If that is so, Piye, you must make peace with Akil and his followers. The people of Egypt and Kush worship him."

Piye broke free of her grasp. "You see, that is the problem!"

Suddenly, they could hear tantara and cheering from outside. Piye's face transformed from anger to excitement as he made his way to the exit. His personal guards followed him. The queen mother watched him leave and returned her gaze to the statue of Shabaka.

Piye stood on the stone-paved road, surrounded by his armed guards. From his vantage point, he could see Gahiji riding proudly in his chariot with Abayomi next to him. The musims followed him on their horses. They were in full regalia as thousands of onlookers cheered Piye's name. The blare of trumpets announced a hero's welcome. Somehow, the people knew. Abayomi looked on, nervously.

Fadil and Catena were deep into their game of Senet, a boardgame using small tokens and miniature figurines on a decorative boxlike, checkered board. They decided to partake in the game after touring the gardens that day. Catena's assiduous study of the game made her a quick learner of the Egyptian game. Fadil occasionally roweled her to throw her off her game.

The dwelling they played was a lotusland purchased by Fadil as Catena's new living quarters. It was in the affluent sector of Napata and had a guarded entry, a wide array of flora, and a beautiful, balustrade veranda that overlooked a serenity pond. Sunlight streaked through the latticed windows of the spacious bungalow. The room was furnished with extravagant décor of Etruscan origin.

"What if I move this piece here?" Catena said with a quizzical look.

"You must let your tokens determine your move," Fadil answered. "That pawn is not your best move, all considered."

Fadil enjoyed watching her in her delectation. He enjoyed admiring her golden skin, her sable hair, and her almond eyes. His eyes' attention was distracted by her shapely figure, sheathed in a satin, violet gown.

"I am pleased you decided to stay," Fadil said unexpectedly. "Are you aware that this game began in my homeland?"

"I have reason to stay, and no, I did not," Catena said 139

with an amiable smirk. "I believe I have won."

Fadil's eyesight shifted from her to the board. "You sneaky snake! You distracted me on purpose. Son of Seth."

Catena started laughing and kissed Fadil on the lips. Their lips locked in complete bliss. They were interrupted by the knock on the door. "Enter!" Fadil never looked away from Catena to acknowledge the guard.

"The chief advisor has been requested by the pharaoh," the man said without emotion.

"Wait for me in the hall," Fadil snapped back.

As the guard closed the door behind him, Catena noticed five guards standing outside the door. Fadil sighed, and Catena countered with a smile. This was done looking upwards since he was considerably taller.

"It must be very important," she said.

"An important person has arrived," he replied. "I will see you at the Hour of the Toad?"

Catena nodded. Fadil smiled and adjusted his khopesh. He left with the guards trailing behind him. Catena put the game away and poured herself a goblet of wine. She sipped and thought of Fadil, favorably. Her father had returned to Messana, and she decided to stay in Napata. Catena was ruminating over Fadil when there was a knock at the door, once again. She thought Fadil had forgotten something when she opened the door. Alas, it was the shadowy, robed man that visited Fadil on several occasions. This time, he 140 had a face. He had very pale skin, sunken eyes, and a goatee. His face was as interesting as mud.

"You seem surprised," he whispered in Aramaic.

"How did you find me?"

"It is good that you have bonded with the brother," he continued. "King Sargon has been very kind to your father, Catena. How long his generosity endures depends on your actions. Have you forgotten your task?"

"No," Catena said as she lowered her head. "I will follow through with what has to be done."

Chapter Seventeen

Piye welcomed them in his throne room with open arms. A contingent of personal guards, Bahiti, Fadil, Rashidi, and several vassals were in attendance. He stood as Gahiji entered the large, torchlit chamber. Abayomi and several musims followed the Egyptian warrior. Gahiji took a knee, bowed his head, and unsheathed his khopesh. He placed the blade on the floor.

"Gahiji, my friend, it has been too long," Piye said with excitement. "How fortuitous it was the day I received your victory."

"May Osiris carry you, my pharaoh," Gahiji said sternly. "As you can see, I have fulfilled your wishes, once again."

"Stand, my friend." Piye approached Gahiji and hugged him. "You never disappoint me, Gahiji." Piye gazed over his shoulder. "I see you still have women in your ranks."

"They can be capable warriors when needed," Gahiji said with a smile.

Piye raised a hand in the air. "My life is much too precious. You are far too trusting, Gahiji." Piye knelt before a nervous Abayomi. "I have searched for you for a very long time, son." He stood and gestured to his family. "This is Bahiti. She is your mother and queen. This is your uncle, Fadil. He is quite unimpressive, but I am sure you will learn to love him, regardless. And the rest, you will learn to avoid." Piye chuckled.

Abayomi stared silently at the middle-aged pharaoh. He noticed the resemblance in their almond-shaped eyes and small, compact frames. He noticed the long battle scar that ran horizontal on his chest.

"Let us catch up," Piye said playfully. "Everyone, leave!" He grabbed Gahiji's arm and whispered, "There is another problem that requires your special skillset. We will discuss later."

Gahiji nodded and sheathed his weapon. Everyone departed the chamber, except for Piye and Abayomi. Father and son stared at one another, Piye in complete bliss, Abayomi in complete fear.

"Sit beside me, son," Piye said with hand extended. "I want to instruct you on how to rule."

^^^

Gahiji escorted Bahiti to her private chamber. After dismissing her ladies-in-waiting, Bahiti opened the door and entered. Gahiji followed. They embraced immediately and began kissing aggressively. They were very solicitous about their love affair. It was unknown what Piye would do if he were to ever discover their adulterous history.

Bahiti broke away. "My husband is unhinged. We can no longer continue this."

"You mean brother," Gahiji snapped. "Has he the right to deny our love?"

"No," Bahiti said. "He has the right to have us both set afire."

"Not if I kill him."

"You would kill a man you have known for ages? You have served Piye since childhood!"

"For you, yes," Gahiji said as he moved closer. "You know he is not fit to be your king, our ruler, your husband."

"Nonetheless, he is my husband and pharaoh," Bahiti said as she looked away. "That is what the gods command."

"And if he perishes in battle? I understand that the Assyrians are preparing to invade."

"How many times has Piye gone to battle? How many times has he died? It is an improbable conclusion."

Gahiji caressed her cheek. "A spear is harder to evade when it comes from behind."

Bahiti held his hand to her face. "Piye is the spear."

^^^

Piye leaned towards Abayomi. "Your grandfather told me that it requires a man to go beyond his limits to rule Egypt. One must be willing to sacrifice all that he cherished to maintain complete subjugation. I was no older than you."

"Where is my mother?" Abayomi said with an indignant tone.

"I do not know. Mosi was a complicated woman. You will find that many women tend to be complicated. Always remember, it is easier to love your country than your wife."

Abayomi stood. "She is hiding from you, isn't she? You want to kill her?"

Piye's face expressed his sadness. "I loved your mother more than you could possibly imagine. I offered her my heart, and she chose to flee after you were conceived, relinquishing me from my rightful heir."

"I do not belong here," Abayomi said as he lowered his head.

Piye lifted Abayomi's head by the chin. "Have you ever ridden a horse?"

Shortly thereafter, Abayomi sat behind Piye atop Kawa. As Kawa raced through the courtyard, Piye held the reins tightly. Abayomi clenched Piye's waist as the horse galloped through open field. Dust rose and irritated Abayomi's eyes. As dusk drew near, Abayomi began unveiling a smile. His initial fear transformed into excitement. Piye kicked the stallion's belly as it negotiated the final obstacle, leaping effortlessly over the hurdle. Abayomi succumbed to laughter as Kawa slowed. Piye peeked over his shoulder and grinned.

^^^

Nuri was just across the Nile from Napata, and Piye could see the mining village from his chamber's veranda. The night was still and bitter with a slight zephyr cascading off the wide waterway. He could see the silhouette of a vil- 145 lage that was quiet and fast asleep. He sipped his goblet of wine as the fire erupted. It soon became a glowing blaze. The screams of men rushing to extinguish the flames and women gathering the children echoed through the winds. Sparks from rising ember appeared as common fireflies in mating season. The origin of this unfathomable horror would stay hidden to the people. Piye took another sip of libation, smiled, and was soon abed, sleeping peacefully.

Chapter Eighteen

First harvest had begun, and the farmers reaped their bountiful crops throughout the lower kingdom. What was typically a festive season was tainted by the undertones of war. On the night prior to the two-week long celebration of Osiris and his blessings, Piye prepared for the upcoming battle. The pharaoh and his warriors knelt before the mighty Nile and drank the blood of slaughtered mares. Each man passed the cup and prayed for victory or an honorable death. As they drank their paganistic fluid, a few of the warriors carved ink into their faces. Murky blood dripped from their chins and dissolved in the sands beneath their feet. Priests stood next to torchlight, chanting text from the days retired to legends. Piye gazed at Fadil and gave him a reassuring smirk.

"The gods smile upon the fearless," Piye whispered in Meroitic.

"The gods are without fault," Fadil responded.

"We are called upon, once again," Piye said harmoniously.

"We will not be defeated. We will not be distraught," Fadil said.

"The gods care not the words of man," they said in unison.

The next morning, Piye and his army were embarking

on four quinqueremes. His immediate army consisted of two thousand infantry, two thousand archers and slingers, and two thousand horsemen and chariots. Another one thousand infantry was to be provided by King Alara. As men and neighing horses boarded the large ships, Piye said his goodbyes to his mother, wife, and friend. Along with his kepresh headdress, he wore his leather tunic, clad in iron pieces from Kushite mines. His sandals were laced with iron straps. It was an overcast day, yet falcons soared through the clouds while announcing their presence.

"Keep Abayomi safe, mother," Piye said with a slight bow. "This should take but a moment."

The queen mother held his hands. "We will pray for your return, Piye. "You must keep safe as well. I cannot lose my son as I lost my husband. You were always a selfish boy."

Piye's smile was met by Bahiti's scorn. "Fret not, mother. Piye is a skillful warrior and a god." She smiled, bowed, and walked away.

Before Piye could react, Gahiji lowered his head and gritted his teeth. "I should be your vanguard, my pharaoh. I am twice the fighter of Fadil."

Piye placed a hand upon his shoulder. "I know you are our best defender, which is why I am leaving you in charge. You shall be regent in my stead."

"Yes, my pharaoh," Gahiji said confidently.

Piye chuckled and leaned close. "Try not to murder anyone," Piye whispered in his ear.

Piye gave him two pats on the shoulder and headed for his quinquereme, escorted by twenty spearmen. Gahiji caught a glimpse of Fadil boarding as well. The two men exchanged heated stares until Fadil entered the deck of the oar-powered battleship.

^^^

As the vessels moved up the Nile, Piye met with Fadil and five officers below deck. The candlelit cabin had sufficient lighting to evaluate their plan of attack. Items on the rustic table slid gently with each surge of the Nile. The quinqueremes glided on the dark river like alligators searching for prey. They were passing Aswan and entered the upper kingdom. It would take two more days before they could disembark at Cairo.

"King Alara will be ready with his army of two thousand men, my pharaoh," one officer said while studying a battle map. "My pharaoh, will King Kashta accompany us as well?"

"He has other duties given to him," Piye said before sipping his goblet of red wine.

"The men will be well fed once we reach the pass, my pharaoh," Fadil said from his standing position. "The horses have been properly watered and armored for combat."

Piye sat there, slowly swirling the inebriant. He then smelled the wine and took another sip. "The northerners do know their grapes."

"Shall we increase oar power, my pharaoh?" another of- 149

ficer offered. "We could add more slaves and reach Cairo in half the time."

Piye stared closely at the map. "No. We will disembark at Sais," Piye said while tracing the route with his index finger. "Spies are usually where you most expect them to be. Besides, I want them to arrive first and take comfort in the high ground."

"As you wish, my pharaoh."

"Leave us. I want to be alone with my brother."

Immediately, the officers gathered their paraphernalia and exited the room. Piye gestured to Fadil to sit. He placed an empty goblet before his younger brother and poured wine into the glass. Spillage was occurring as expected from the motion of the vessel.

"It has been too long since we shared a drink together, Fadil. Tonight, let us conversate as banter brothers."

"We will not see the true might of the Assyrians, Piye," Fadil said before sipping the wine. He looked as uncomfortable as a dog with wings. Fadil was not a drinker.

"Sargon will take me lightly," Piye said as he nodded. "How dare he put me to the test!"

Fadil drank and set the goblet down. "Perhaps, he feels you are more careless than father."

Piye nodded. "Yet, father kept the godless creatures out of Egypt, did he not?"

"Regardless, heed mother's words, Piye," Fadil replied.

"Ignore the words of an old woman, Fadil," Piye said with a slight smirk. "A warrior must fling caution to the wind. Mother concerns me."

Fadil drank more. His inhibitions abandoned his conscience. He felt calm, a feeling he rarely experienced. Fadil took another drink before setting the goblet down, clumsily. "Piye, why do you despise me?"

Piye's face morphed into a look of disdain. "Fadil, you will face death soon. Is that the question which entangles you?"

Fadil stumbled to his feet, nearly toppling his goblet. "I will check on the men before retiring." He made his way to the door, slightly inebriated. "May Osiris carry you, brother."

"He will carry us all," Piye said in a matter-of-fact tone. "Fadil, I do not despise you. I want you to be worthy of sharing father's blood."

Fadil nodded, smiled, and exited the cabin. Piye clenched his lips after finishing his wine. He stood and pointed at the Assyrian force on the battle map.

"Sargon, we finally meet."

^^^

Piye and his army faced the Assyrian army at Sinai Pass, a narrow passageway that opened south of an estuary linking the Red Sea and the Mediterranean Sea. The sweltering sun flew above the lush, eastern hillside. Sweat poured down the faces of every warrior. On both sides were hills that overlooked the five-hundred-yard battlefield. King Alara's foot soldiers stood with Piye's, increasing his army size by two thousand. Opposing them were the Assyrians, seven thousand heavy and light infantry, two thousand horsemen, and two thousand archers occupying the hills. The infantry was armed with a spears and longswords and protected by conical iron helmets, leather body armor, and a shield.

It was the Assyrian archers who instilled fear in the region. Armored less cumbersome than the typical, infantry soldier, the archers carried a variety of bows, including the composite bow. Deadly accurate, their arrows were often of the flaming type.

The Assyrian horsemen were also rightfully infamous and skilled. They were renowned for riding sturdier, heavier horses, and they mastered the art of mounted, lance attack. They used their longswords as secondary weapons.

"Hm, I fail to see Sargon among the sheep herders," Piye said to the officers mounted behind him.

Piye stroked Kawa's mane from his saddle. He positioned his command station and a detachment of personal guards behind the infantry and between his archers and slingers. Each infantry warrior carried a large wooden shield that was encased in cowhide. Each man was armed with a khopesh and a short spear. For armor, they wore linseed breastplates, iron bracers, and a waist shield of thick fabric. They completed the ensemble with iron helms resembling a jackal, the idolatry that followed Anubis.

The archers and slingers were of a different ilk. They preferred a limited amount of armor as to not restrict their loading and release motions. The muscular men wore their tunic bottoms and fabric headdresses only. The archers were skilled in the longbow, an accurate, deadly weapon from a considerable distance. A quiver of arrows at their feet solidified their lethalness. The slingers were very effective with their projectile weapons and sling bullets, small stones of high density.

Each war chariot was manned by a driver to control the horse with two leather reins and a warrior to impale foes with a spear or launch arrows from a composite bow. Just as the chariot itself, both men were armored with light, bronze plate to increase the war machine's fleetness. The horsemen followed suit. At the wheelbase of each two-wheeled chariot were spinning blades to remedy all encircling opposers.

Fadil commanded the chariots. He donned his iron helmet, a symbolic nemes of the Sphinx. The facial plate gave the wearer a stoic, almost frightening, aura. He moved his chariot to the front of the horse regiment. Dust was at his wake.

"Osiris is with us, warriors," Fadil shouted as he tightened the reins of his neighing horse. "If not, he will greet you in Duat!"

The men cheered and began their battle cries. It soon spread to the infantry and reached Piye's ears. The Assyrians countered with their deep bellows that reverberated throughout the battlefield. Piye unsheathed his khopesh and pointed it forward. The blare of trumpets began the Egyptian advance and commanded his forces to engage the 153

Assyrians. The battle had begun.

The Egyptian infantry marched forward quickly in a phalanx, their shields protecting a few from the barrage of arrows that hit them from above. Some of the arrows found their marks, penetrating armor and flesh. Several fell before engaging the Assyrians sprinting their direction. Blood mist pervaded the air and flowed profusely from limbs and heads of the hapless. Eventually, shields clashed, and the clangor of arms rang across the battlefield. The Assyrian heavy infantry impaled with their long spears. The khopesh met the longsword. Arrows continued to rain down from both armies indiscriminately. Officers shouted commands as many heroic warriors inhaled their final lungful of life.

The chariots charged forward with Fadil at the tip of the armored cavalry. The neighing of horses blanketed the collision of horses and chariots. The chariots sliced through the Assyrian horsemen with ease. The wheel-blades dismembered steeds that attempted to pass, causing horsemen into a sudden dismount and impaling. However, the chariots were still a target for the hillside archers. Their arrows still filled the sky. The Egyptian archers shifted their aim to the Assyrian bowmen in retaliation. Controlled chaos ensued, and havoc ruled the day.

"You are too close to the edge," Fadil screamed to the man sharing his chariot.

The man was leaning to release an arrow after another. Fadil pulled the reins to the left suddenly to avoid an oncoming Assyrians horseman with a long spear, causing the horse displeasure from the yoke. The sudden evasion jolted the armored carriage, which propelled the other warrior over the side. He was able to grasp the carriage's edge. Instinctively, Fadil grabbed the man's forearm to no avail. The man slipped from Fadil's grasp and plummeted to his death beneath the carriage's large, spoked wheels. Fadil shrieked and turned his focus back to regaining control of the horse leading the heavy chariot. Alas, it was too late. His chariot collided with a fallen Assyrian stallion.

Fadil was thrown from the crashing chariot and landed on his back, losing his helmet in the process. He swallowed a clump of dirt that covered his face and body as well. Pain resonated from his neck to his thighs. When he opened his eyes, a cluster of arrows were streaming downward. His visceral reaction was to roll and avoid being impaled. Even though a sharp pain throbbed throughout his frame and blood poured from his forehead, Fadil regained his footing and unsheathed his khopesh. He was surrounded by melee and ruthless massacre. He noticed that his chariot was splinters and his horse was floundering on the ground, crying.

"In the name of Sargon!" an Assyrian warrior with a spear raced at Fadil from behind.

Fadil did not budge. He stood there and stared at the gritty warrior. As the man moved closer, Fadil faced him with his sword hand at his waist. As the Assyrian raised his spear to skewer Fadil, he never anticipated the chariot from the right that trampled him to death, leaving a pile of flesh, bones, and blood. Fadil took several deep breaths and espied his surroundings until he noticed an arrow protruding from his shoulder. He witnessed men on both sides being cut to pieces. Men called for their gods and mothers. Dust swirled and blood splattered, making the battlefield a crimson nightmare. The utter fear, turmoil, and pain overwhelmed him, and Fadil collapsed unconscious on the spot. 155

As the screams and clangor of battle continued, Piye scanned the battlefield, perched atop Kawa. He dismounted and took a knee. He rubbed his stubbly chin and stared indirectly at the sun. "The winds blow in both directions, yet they are indiscernible."

A key vassal on horseback appeared perplexed. "Forgive me, my pharaoh. Would it serve us better to fall back and counterattack under the cover of darkness?"

"The gods betray those who prolong inevitability," Piye said. "Tell me, do you believe the gods are with us?"

The vassal hesitated before responding. "Yes, my pharaoh."

Piye stood and rubbed his hands gently to cleanse his hands of grime. "The gods could care less about us." Piye stared at the vassal. "Fortunately, I am with us."

Suddenly, a wave of a thousand Cimmerian warriors assaulted the eastern hilltop. The nomadic horsemen were of Scythian stock and were a thorn in Assyrian-rule. They wielded bronze sabers and donned light leather armor. Speed of horse was their tactic in battle, and they rode their stallions with the ferocity of a sand-carrying windstorm. They were fierce and an ally to Piye's Egypt.

Simultaneously, a thousand Etruscan spearmen flooded the western hilltop, led by Kashta. Piye had sent him to negotiate a quid pro quo with King Romulus. Their men utilized short spears for hurling at their enemies with great accuracy. Wearing little to no armor, each man from Etruria fought bravely for their king and personal wealth.

Both Assyrian archer regiments were overwhelmed and began retreating. Many were decapitated or speared before having a chance to flee. In time, the entire Assyrian force were scattered in complete disarray, and the Egyptians gave chase for a mile. This pleased Piye.

After the battle, the remaining Egyptian army began loading their dead onto carts for return to Napata. They would receive a proper burial. The Assyrian dead were placed in a pyre and burned. Several Assyrians were captured, only to be kept in servitude. Piye and his officers assessed the aftermath, stepping over the fallen and the wounded approaching death. Through the fog of battle, Kashta approached Piye with a huge smile. He was caked in the blood of others and appeared weary. Piye and Kashta embraced.

"You fought well, Kashta," Piye said.

Kashta bowed. "All in your glory, my pharaoh. May Osiris carry you."

Piye put his hand on his friend's shoulder. He returned his smile and continued pass the king of Thebes. "I knew you would not fail to serve me. Thank you for your service, friend."

Kashta nodded and gazed at the hazy sky. He took pleasure in knowing he was able to broker a deal with the Etruscans, a fledgling people. His smile soon dissipated into a look of astonishment as three arrows pierced his chest. Blood poured from his mouth and nose as he dropped to his knees. He attempted to utter a final word before collapsing to his death. Piye had never forgotten his betrayal.

157

Piye found Fadil stumbling while holding his wounded shoulder. Piye helped steady his younger brother. The officers dispersed to support their wounded as well.

"You fought well," Piye said as he patted Fadil's back. "Osiris and Horus are with us."

"In time, I will be with them," Fadil said while wincing.

"Whatever does not kill you will be very painful," Piye said. "You can endure."

They walked slowly towards the silhouette of the distant Sphinx. By all accounts, the battle was a resounding victory for the pharaoh. However, Piye knew Sargon was a pragmatic leader and was willing to sacrifice a few thousand to gauge his opponent's true strength. A light skirmish occurred that evening, and the Assyrian counterattack was repelled as well. The Assyrians would return in greater numbers, and Piye planned to be prepared.

"Fadil, I know of your deception," Piye said as he stared at the horizon. "I know of the Sicilian harlot as well. I see everything."

"What?" Fadil said, confused by his brother's latter remark.

Fadil was taken aback. He was left speechless. Before he could manifest a reason or an excuse, Piye wandered away from Fadil in callous fashion.

Chapter Nineteen

Chenzira and Abayomi had just gathered the day's catch and piled the fish next to their campfire. The sun had kissed the horizon, making the sky reddish gold. Desert owls sounded their presence, and the Nile's hills were crisp and breezy. Chenzira reached for a bucket of river water, started gutting a fish, and dipped the perch for cleansing.

"What are you doing?" Abayomi inquired.

"I am cleaning the fish to eat," Chenzira said while cutting vigorously. "There are times when fire is a luxury, and you must eat the fish raw. You will like it."

Abayomi had a look of disgust. "I will put the fish I caught over fire." He began skewering a perch on a large twig.

Chenzira stood and smacked the stick from his grasp. "Abayomi, you must learn to do without. There are times when only malleable men survive a difficult situation."

Abayomi picked up the twin and continued preparing the fish to be grilled. "I will avoid a difficult situation by not getting sick."

"Some things are unavoidable."

Abayomi awoke to tears and remembered quickly where he slept that night. His first impression of the dimly lit chamber was that it was fit for a girl. Silk sheets lined the bedding. Velvet drapes hung from the picturesque windows. Various paintings of common Egyptian flora decorated the walls. A hearth was in the center of the room. He was alone in the spacious chamber.

Abayomi stood and espied his surroundings. He felt some reassurance that he still was wearing his dingy tunic and sandals. He treaded softly to the large, wooden door. He peeked into the empty corridor. Seeing that the coast was clear, he tried to make his escape. Abayomi was confident he would secure his freedom until he turned the corner. Bahiti stood there with an escort of handmaidens. For a moment, they stared at each other, Bahiti with anger and Abayomi with fear.

"You may decide to leave after your morning lessons," Bahiti said stoically. "If that is your desire at that time, I could care less."

Bahiti veered around and walked down the torchlit corridor, followed by her handmaidens, who carried Bahiti's cloak bottom behind her. Abayomi took a deep swallow and proceeded behind her. He held tightly to his mother's coin.

^^^

Gahiji slid into his role as regent, comfortably. The robed high priests of the Osiris, Isis, Horus, Re, Ptah, Anubis, Hathor, Bastet, Thoth, Amon, and Seth factions shared the spiritual, council chamber with him. Several of Piye's vassals offered their insights as well. Torches flickered in the spacious room with each subtle breeze. An assortment of parchment littered the giant wooden table of rustic carvings and idolatry. Gahiji had two musims guarding the entrance for a purely intimidating presence. The sight of Akil at the meeting made Gahiji more irritable than normal.

"It is decided. Taxes are to be gathered on the fourth moon," Gahiji said while shuffling scrolls. "Ship construction cannot be delayed."

"It will begin, immediately," Rashidi said as he pressed the ink-stained stone to several of the parchments. "I have requested each king construct a shrine in honor of the gods, in addition to a healthy contingent each of trained warriors."

"Our coffers have been bilked of their full capacity due to the lack of grain production," Gahiji added. "We must incentivize our farmers to increase output."

"And what of the ten pyramids promised to us by the pharaoh? The gods must be appeased." Ralia said in a snarky tone. The high priestess of Isis could not hide her frustration.

Gahiji sighed. "High priestess, we are at war. Pyramid construction holds little importance. The slaves are needed for fortification purposes."

Ralia leaned back in her chair. "The people should see where their increased taxation is going. If they feel they are funding another war by the pharaoh, they might show their dissatisfaction."

"I trust all of you will assist in maintaining the peace."

"Do you?" Akil interceded. "Do you want peace, regent?"

Gahiji smirked and stood. The very sight of Akil infuriated the chief commander to no end. However, he withheld his emotions for the task at hand. He must raise a massive army to thwart the Assyrian threat. Upon Piye's return from battle, Gahiji would have fifty thousand warriors trained and equipped, awaiting marching orders. That was his sole purpose. He would deal with the priest another day.

"Peace begins at Sargon's feet. If he is anything like his father, he will seek to destroy all of Egypt, including the pharaoh, you, me, and our people. Ashes will rise from the plains, and blood will flow up the Nile. If that occurs, priest, whether I want peace or not will be meaningless."

∧∧∧

Abayomi entered the south courtyard of the Pyramid of Great Gatherings, an airy garden of exotic flora and several sandstone fountains. Its lush design and serenity-evoking aura flourished under the midday sunrays cascading through the fortress's opening. Thirty children of various ages sat cross-legged on the stone pavement before the queen mother. They were the offspring of the royal elitist, the children of a future Egypt. As Bahiti joined her mother, Abayomi found an empty spot to huddle beside the other youth. The queen mother continued sharing stories from the past. She spoke eloquently in Old Meroitic.

"What once belonged to Kush, Napata was taken by Thutmose, third of his name. Nearly ten thousand seasons had seen its creation. Of the days of Jebel Barkal and the rise of Amun of Karnak, Shebitku had taken the form of a goose and regained the power of the Kushite with the embrace of Seth. The Pure Mountain gave him the strength

162

and reason to subjugate all of Egypt and reclaim Kush. Napata would be his source of power. Napata would give birth to Shabaka, Abler of the Delta, and Ruler of Kush. Seth had smiled upon Kush and rewarded the pharaoh with Egypt. Shabaka made Napata his home and center of two grand empires. The Temple of Mut and the Temple of Amun remind us of times forgotten."

Abayomi espied his surroundings. The other children sat in awe, waiting on every word uttered by the elderly woman. His eyes locked on one girl of Kushite lineage. The lanky child of ten years smiled his direction. Abayomi was surprised by her amiability and returned an uncomfortable smirk.

"The responsibility has fallen on Piye," the queen mother continued. "He is your pharaoh, Beloved of Amun. He is your father and protector. He is Napata, and Napata is at the heart of Seth. Pay homage, children of Amun. The gods watch over us all. For one day, you will be called upon to carry the Stele of Victory. Never forget those that have sacrificed so much. May Seth give you peace."

^^^

The floral garden was in full bloom, and the reds were vibrant. Fadil noticed that the perennials were uncharacteristically enormous yet unsuspecting. Fadil let his fingertips dance along the lush greenery. This was his mother's garden from long ago. Fadil was of age but was emotionally a child. He felt out of sorts but took solace of that innocent moment. Fadil watched his mother prune several flowers. She spoke to him with her back turned.

"The butterflies return here every harvest. Do you know 163

why they do not fly away, never to return?" She said whimsically.

"No." Fadil's eyes narrowed. He studied the silhouette of the queen mother. She was draped in a dark, silk hooded robe. He could not see her face.

"They will always remember the source of their nourishment. To stray too far away, death is certain."

Fadil moved closer. He lowered her hood, gently. It was Bahiti's face. Although she had the voice of his mother, it seemed normal to Fadil. The apparition that appeared to be his sister extended her palm to allow a monarch butterfly to land in her hand.

"Always remind the people from where their nourishment stems," Bahiti whispered as the butterfly floated away.

Fadil awoke in the cramped quarters of a quinquereme. He felt the waves from below deck as the vessel rocked from side to side. He could hear the groans of the oarsmen chanting with each row. It was night, and Fadil recalled his present whereabouts and state. As he staggered to his feet from the bloodstained cot, he winced. The pain that emanated from his wounded shoulder was fierce. Although his arm was well bandaged and in a sling. Any slight movement caused a throbbing pain. He required fresh air from the damp and dingy cabin. He made his way to the prow.

The center of the Milky Way appeared to hover above the Nile River. The fleet was navigating its way back to Napata. The upper deck was desolate, except for the occasional deckhand. Fadil inhaled the crisp air pummeling his face. He removed the sling and experienced excruciating pain throughout the entire process. As he made a fist, Fadil noticed his brother standing at the bow of the ship. Piye was staring blindly at the night sky. Mist gushed from his mouth. Fadil watched as Piye raised his hands to the heavens, though he could not hear what the pharaoh requested from the gods. Fadil did not want to bring attention to himself. He took refuge in the shadows as the ships glided down the strong current.

Chapter Twenty

Seth sat on his throne and contemplated arrogating his brother's ruling of Duat. The way he saw it, Egypt and the entire universe belonged to him. He transformed from his doglike appearance to human form, a charismatic and commanding being of perfection. He could easily assimilate to the fatuous mortals when he desired. He rubbed his chin in darkness and deliberated on the presumptuous proposal by Isis. He could never forgive Osiris for what was taken from him. He desired to see his brother on his knees and his nephew decapitated.

"The stone is unguarded. Would it be iniquitous to return it in turn? I gave them Kush. I gave them Egypt. My storms ushered in a new kingdom, forged from chaos and purification. I ask that my love, Bastet, guide me in my decision."

Although he had the body of a man, Seth's eyes were still of a canine variety. Fangs began to protrude as slobber dripped down his chin. His hands became yellowish claws. As his anger surfaced, Seth's animalistic tendencies overpowered him.

"Once I regain what is rightfully mine, I will dispense with retribution. Yes, Osiris shall be no more. Isis will assist me in spreading my seed. My children will feed off the carcass of Horus. Re will return to my side. This has been foretold."

Seth severed his wrist with a claw. Ruddy liquid gushed

into the Nile below. The river soon flowed with crimson blood and began overflowing.

"There will never be peace until my brother has fallen. Violence shall shroud the people, and suffering will grow without opposition."

^^^

Piye and his men disembarked in the early morning. Once the pharaoh arrived in Napata, he went immediately to his private stables to groom his steeds. As he brushed the mare he wished to breed with Kawa, Piye remained silent, speaking to no one after his arrival. Three of his personal bodyguards stood by as he began assisting the farrier in horseshoeing their hooves as well. It was his idea of tranquility. It was an escape from the nuisances of people.

After a healthy repast in the garden, Piye went to his personal chamber, bathed, and changed to his casual tunic. He sipped a goblet of wine and stepped onto his veranda that overlooked all of Napata from the Pyramid of Great Gatherings. He took a deep breath and welcomed thousands of onlookers with open arms. His people crowded below, cheering for their pharaoh. Piye let the applause dissipate slowly, soaking in the adulations and servitude.

"People of Napata!" Piye said in his deepest voice. "Did I not promise you victory? The Assyrian scum tried to invade and pollute our lands, and I turned them back. Does Sargon mistake the people of Egypt as sheep he can lead to slaughter? It is a new day. The people have spoken. Kush and Egypt are one. I will take my rightful place among the gods. Our empire shall embrace the fortunes bestowed upon us by the great kings of old. We shall raise an army 167 that will invoke fear for those who seek our demise. I am taking the power of Osiris to Assyria and beyond. The dream of Shabaka shall come to past! I anticipate fear to shatter those who would stand in our way. This is to be!"

Piye exited the veranda to the cheer of thousands. There were a few onlookers who appeared nervous by his words. Two people in particular held hands lowered their heads in prayer from the courtyard below. Bahiti and the queen mother foresaw the arrogance once held by Shabaka.

"My son has forsaken all that is rational," the queen mother muttered.

"Darkness is at our doorstep, I fear," Bahiti said.

^^^

Piye summoned the high priests to his throne room a few days later. As usual, the representative of each sect entered single file. Rashidi was the last to enter the spacious chamber. The walls were lined with spearmen as guards. In unison, they sat at the round table below Piye. The pharaoh sat eloquently with his chin on fist. Gahiji stood behind him.

"My pharaoh, it is good to see you in good health," Rashidi said amiably.

"I wish I shared your optimism, Rashidi," Piye responded immediately.

"The regent is aware of the promise made by you. We must begin constructing the new pyramids," Ralia said as she moved up in her chair. "Put the slaves you boast about to work."

The other priests grunted in agreement to Piye's antipathy. Gahiji grinned at the spiritual puppets, a least in his perception. He gripped the hilt of his khopesh. Piye stood and placed a reassuring palm on his chief commander's shoulder.

"Ralia, you know as well as anybody that we do not receive everything we request," Piye said with a smile. "The gods are funny that way."

"The gods never forget," high priest Akil said. "They will reward those who are true and punish those who are false."

"Ah, Akil, welcome back. It has been too long," Piye said as he began sauntering the room. "I see you were able to escape the terrible fires of Nuri. Has your flock fared the same?"

"We suspect foul play," Akil replied.

Piye stopped and folded his arms. He eyed the elderly man with a look of exasperation. He reached for his goblet of wine, something he always had near him. Piye gulped the libation down and let the vessel fall and rattle across the stone floor.

"I will get to the point," Piye said in a friendly tone. "Your guidance has been most helpful. Truly, all of you are indispensable. However, as Ralia often remarks, I am a living god. So, I ask all of you, why do I need you?"

Suddenly, each spearman pointed his weapon inches

from the heads of the priests. The cries came immediately, and Rashidi cowered like a turtle into its shell. Any attempt to flee was stifled.

"You are to be detained until I see fit you are of use to me. Take them to the pits!"

"Have you gone mad?" Ralia shouted as two guards pulled her away. "The queen mother will never stand for this!"

"I do thank you for your service," Piye said as the priests were dragged away from the chamber.

As Piye left the room, Gahiji nodded and drank from the bottle of wine. He wiped his lips and took another swig. He prepared himself for the turmoil approaching.

^^^

It didn't take long for the queen mother to learn of Piye's transgressions. She made her way down the torchlit corridor, past two guards, and into Pye's private chamber. Infuriate, she walked to within inches of her son, who was taking a sunlit, panoramic view from his balustrade veranda.

"You release the high priests now!" the queen mother demanded. "I will pray for you and appease the gods."

Piye sighed and walked back into the room. He poured himself another goblet of wine and sniffed its contents. "It is time they learned who commands this land."

"You cannot take away the very essence of our people,

Piye. You cannot lockup our only connection to Osiris and eternal life."

"CAN'T I? I AM PHARAOH." Piye slammed his goblet on the floor. "Mother, I ask that you support me in the challenging times."

"I can never support a man that turns his back on the gods, even if he is my son," the queen mother said softly.

"You undermine me to this day. Do you wish to see me fall?" Piye grabbed his forehead in frustration.

The queen mother held tight to the railing, gazed at the people below, and searched within for a peaceful response. "I never wanted to see you fall, Piankhy. Alas, I never wanted to see you rise. You never had the temperament to be pharaoh. I told your father this much. You were meant for grander ways to serve Osiris. I know you are in pain. Perhaps, you were meant to be our highest priest. You are not suited to be pharaoh."

"What do you know of pain?" Piye said with a slight chuckle. "You never embraced our place in Egypt. You are set in the old ways. You never understood the sacrifices made by father and grandfather. Now you insist on polluting my son with that rubbish."

"Sometimes sacrifice requires introspection," the queen mother blurted. "Are you blind? Your search for complete power will kill you, Piye."

Piye clenched his forehead and sighed. He laughed as he made his way back to the veranda. He caressed her shoulders and continued to smile. "Fret not, I will see fa- 171 ther's dream to fruition."

She returned his smile with her own. The queen mother stroked his cheek as tears rolled down hers. In that moment, Piye emotionally cracked and shoved her over the railing to her screaming death. Piye peeked over the edge to ensure his act of matricide was complete.

Chapter Twenty-One

"You do not know my brother," Fadil shouted at Catena. "You are in danger. I have my most trusted men to escort you south. Remain there until it is safe."

Catena paced her lavish quarters in a slight panic. She hadn't seen Fadil for months, and she was startled by his sudden, panic-stricken visit. She was preparing for the night as demonstrated by her nightgown and long, dark hair in a bun.

"It is time to complete your promise to Sargon," Catena said as she held Fadil.

Fadil pushed her away. "What madness do you speak?"

Catena grabbed him by the waist. "What started as another mission is now love. I am not who I appear. I was sent here to make sure that it is done."

Fadil lurched back and unsheathed his khopesh. "You are an Assyrian spy?"

"I wish to save my blood," she replied. "Sargon has my father. You must help me by fulfilling your promise. That is why you must sacrifice your brother to save the people of Egypt. Sargon will be ruthless, otherwise."

"I was just a bitter soul when I made such a foolish promise!" Fadil said in retrospect. He calmed his nerves. "I can help your father."

173

"Yes, you can," Catena said as she circumvented the blade and held him once more. "Piye must perish. You know that deep in your heart."

BOOM! BOOM!

A knock at the chamber door stopped their conversation. Fadil put a finger over her mouth gently. He pointed his sword at the heavy, wooden door as he approached the source of knocking, cautiously.

"Announce yourself!"

"Chief Advisor, I have an urgent message."

Fadil opened the door, recognizing the sound of his guard's voice. Two soldiers stood in the torchlit corridor and bowed before their commander. Fadil espied the hallway quickly.

"It is about the queen mother," the soldier uttered.

^^^

Fadil gathered fifteen of his most trusted warriors to accompany him to Piye's private chamber. As they marched down the dark hallway leading to the chamber, they were met by Gahiji and twenty musims. Fadil and his men stopped and grabbed the hilts of their swords.

"The pharaoh wishes to be alone at this time, Chief Advisor," Gahiji said smugly as his men blocked the closed chamber door.

174   Fadil unsheathed his khopesh. "Move away, Gahiji.

This does not concern you!"

The musims followed suit and unsheathed their swords in unison. Fadil's men unsheathed their sickle-shaped swords as well. Gahiji drew his khopesh.

"He may pay for his wickedness but not by you, Fadil," Gahiji said in an antagonistic tone. "Return when your brother has finished mourning."

"Move aside, Gahiji," Fadil said. "Move aside, or you will be moved."

Gahiji chuckled. "You really must learn to forget. She was not the puritan you make her out to be."

"Very well, today you die," Fadil said as he pointed his blade at Gahiji.

"Poor Fadil, forever searching for purpose," Gahiji said as he ran his index finger along his khopesh's sharp end. "Musims, this is my battle. Do not interfere."

Fadil gestured to his men to stand down. "This has been a long time coming."

"Yes, I would agree, Kushite," Gahiji said as he took a defensive posture.

Fadil pounced on him immediately. Their swords connected, and the clangor of melee reverberated throughout the narrow hallway. Fadil attempted to slash Gahiji across the abdomen. The chief commander evaded it easily and countered with a downward strike across Fadil's midsection, which Fadil repelled with precision. They were fight- 175 ing for blood. They were fighting with unresolved bitterness. The men surrounded them, creating a human arena. Gahiji rolled and swung for Fadil's legs. With uncanny stealth, Fadil leapfrogged the swipe and punched Gahiji in the mouth. However, Fadil forgot his wounded shoulder that was very much still healing. He grimaced as he recoiled for another strike.

Gahiji wiped the blood that trickled from his mouth. "I heard you were very effective in combat, but this is not the battlefield. This is vengeance unhindered."

In one seamless motion, Gahiji unveiled a dagger from beneath his leather bracer and hurled it at Fadil. The blade pierced his thigh, causing Fadil to collapse to the floor in excruciating pain. Before Fadil could recollect his thoughts and sword, Gahiji's blade was inches from the chief advisor's neck.

"I rarely find pleasure in death, but this will be quite satisfying," Gahiji whispered as he raised his khopesh for the deathblow.

"Gahiji!" Bahiti said as she maneuvered through the crowd of men. "He is my brother."

Immediately, Gahiji and every man in the corridor fell to one knee. "The Great Royal Wife," they shouted in unison.

Bahiti approached Gahiji and placed a palm on his pate. "We must give our mother a proper burial."

Gahiji nodded and stood. He sheathed his khopesh and exited the area in silence. His musims remained on guard.

Fadil attempted to stand to no avail. He felt the blood streaming down his leg and the throbbing from his shoulder. He stayed down breathing heavily.

"Remember, our blood must always endure," Bahiti said as she walked past her younger brother. "Your death serves no purpose."

Chapter Twenty-Two

The pits were the former kennels where Pharaoh Shabaka raised various hounds during his reign. However, Piye was not an admirer of the canine species. Alas, he had them converted to his personal dungeon for those who disappointed the pharaoh. The space was located beneath the stables. It was dank, dark, and teeming with fungus.

Piye relished the opportunity to visit his newly acquired prisoners that evening. As he strolled the murky, barred cells with two guards, Piye relied on his escorts to illuminate the narrow corridor with their torches. The indistinguishable inhabitants were fast asleep in makeshift bedding. The place reeked of manure and earth.

"My pharaoh?" a voice whispered.

They stopped and focused their torches at one cell. Piye squinted his eyes to see a beleaguered man approach the bars. He was dirty, unshaven, and limping. The man was Rashidi.

"Rashidi, the gods do not look well upon you," Piye said with a smirk.

"The gods look upon man with great disdain, my pharaoh," Rashidi uttered in discomfort. "It is my sovereign's disdain I have unleashed. I inquire as to my liege's cruelty."

Piye leaned in. "Rashidi, I never trusted you. My father

believed you were our link to the underworld. I believe you are the most spineless opportunist. A man who never disagrees is too malleable to support you when needed."

The chubby, Egyptian priest clenched the bars of his cells. "Userkaf perished in a prison of similar design. Was it at the behest of Osiris himself?"

"I care not," Piye said as he shrugged.

"My pharaoh, if it is your pleasure, may I return to my duties of serving Osiris and ensuring your family reigns for a thousand years?"

"Your destiny has not been decided. Life is facetious that way." Piye winked and continued his stroll.

He reached the cell that held Ralia, an abyss like Rashidi's. Piye approached the bars to get a closer view of the high priestess of Isis cowering in a murky corner. The petite, elderly woman stood and tightened her ceremonial robe. Ralia maintained a pretentious appearance in her destitute state. Her hair was disheveled, and she was barefoot.

"Ralia, I did not wish this for you," Piye said with an apologetic tone. "Swear loyalty to me and diminish your pious ways. I am the way to the truth."

"You are the worm that devours an apple to its root," Ralia replied. "You are no god."

Piye sighed. "You were always one for a dramatic tale for a simple response. Out of respect to my father, I can make you my head priestess."

"The Divine Mourner has foreseen your death, my pharaoh," Ralia said as she chuckled. "Do you want to know of your passing?"

Piye became agitated. "I am immortal!"

"Even gods are slaves to the underworld," Ralia whispered. "We are all simply the dolls that exist in the heavens. That is where loyalty is sworn, Piye."

Piye and Ralia came face to face at the metal bars. Piye took a deep breath and exhaled, emphatically. Their eyes met, and they stared forcefully at one another. It was Ralia who taught him the histories of Egypt's past. She gave Piye the foundation for understanding the omnipotence of Osiris. He credited her for his soul.

"Why must you tear at my heart?" Piye said with exasperation. "Tell me. How will I die?"

"Even as a child, you were blind to the limitations of power and the shortcomings of mortals," Ralia said under her breath. "You will not perish alone, my pharaoh. Someone you love will accompany you to Duat."

"Is that so?" Piye said with a smirk.

"That is so," she replied.

Piye gritted his teeth and stormed away. His guards followed as he exited the dark cavern. Ralia chortled until Piye disappeared in the shadows. She relished in Piye's frustration and obvious fear.

Abayomi wiped the grains of sand from his lips as he picked himself up from the training room ground, an outdoor platform outside the antechamber of the Pyramid of Great Gatherings. It was where the musims trained. It was where Gahiji was teaching the prince the art of close combat.

"Keep your eyes on your opponent's feet," Gahiji said as he pointed his wooden sword at Abayomi. "Their eyes may deceive you. Your opponent's feet have a mind of their own."

Abayomi grabbed his wooden sword from the ground. "I am not a warrior."

"That is what your friend said when I captured him," Gahiji said with a sinister undertone.

Abayomi launched his small frame at Gahiji. He swung the wooden weapon, and Gahiji evaded the blow. The momentum of Abayomi's weight propelled the boy to the ground, once more. Gahiji tapped him on the shoulder with the dull blade of his practice weapon.

"There is no room for anger in combat," Gahiji said unsympathetically. "Think of it as a business transaction. You want your opponent dead. He wants to stay alive. It is that simple."

Abayomi stood and patted the grime from his tunic. Sweat poured down his brow. "When I am pharaoh, I will kill you!"

"That is your prerogative, prince," Gahiji replied. "However, you will need to learn how to swing a sword 181 until that moment. Again! This time, hold your sword at your midriff to disguise your attack."

Abayomi attempted a thrust attack to no avail. Gahiji simply parried his attack and hurled the boy to the ground. Abayomi landed on his backside and grimaced. The unforgiving dirt provided a sharp pain upon his hindquarters. His dreadlocks were covered in dust. Frustrated, the boy slammed his palms on the ground and began weeping.

"It takes time, prince," Gahiji said empathetically. "However, I will train you, to kill me if necessary."

Abayomi's crying transformed slowly into a slight chortle. He stood, dusted himself off, and held his weapon in preparation for another engagement. He held his sword at his midsection with a determined posture. Gahiji grinned.

^^^

Bahiti stared at the coffin in utter sadness. It contained her mother. The opening of the mouth ceremony had been performed by junior priests; a ritual handled normally by a high priest. Nonetheless, the mummification process was complete, and the body was encased in a golden sarcophagus that idolized Seth, the god of chaos. Until the construction of the queen mother's burial pyramid was completed, she remained prone in her favorite place of serenity while she lived, her garden. Bahiti stood there alone, surrounded by lush greenery, burning incense, and the cawing of birds overhead. Until which time, the mummy will be carried to the burial chamber, where it will reside for eternity.

182   Bahiti knelt and began a silent prayer. After requesting

that Isis allows her mother to enter Duat, Bahiti began crying profusely. It was as though the pain she had endured, over the years, had reemerged as an uncontrollable flame. She rested her hands on the coffin and gazed at the heavens.

"You are beside father. The Hour Vigil was magnanimous. Nobles attended from the far reaches of the land. Nephthys shined for all in her presence. I pray that Osiris judges you to be kind and pure of heart. I cannot say the same of my other brethren."

At that moment, a monarch butterfly floated over Bahiti and landed on the sarcophagus. As its wings fluttered, Bahiti eyes were locked on the beautiful insect. Bahiti brushed aside her long braids and reached for the butterfly with her index finger. The butterfly flew and landed miraculously on her finger. She spoke in ancient Meroitic.

"We are all but the remains of those who have risen before Amun. He chooses to lift the righteous and to punish those who have forgotten his wisdom. It is the way of the humbled to follow impetuously."

Chapter Twenty-Three

The Bones of Menes once stood as an Egyptian stronghold until it fell under the assimilation by Shebitku and the Kush Empire. It stood east of Kerma and was a skeleton of its strength. Hence its new name. Indeed, what before was the Egyptian pharaoh's southern fortress had become ruins of crumbling stone and eerie surroundings. Only the walls of the structure remained. In its center were six, limestone pillars in a circular pattern. At the foot of each cylindrical sat a king and their chief vassal for each kingdom within the Egyptian empire, King Bebti of Khmun, King Alara of Cairo, King Ottah of Thebes, King Sadiki of Abu Simbel, and King Ur Atim of Khartoum. The final pillar was reserved for its final member, the pharaoh. The sky was bright and clear, giving way to a zephyr of warmness on occasion.

Piye arrived in customary fashion. He was carried on a palanquin by several slaves. The litter-like transporter was cloaked in silk and held an additional passenger, Abayomi. They both wore bejeweled tunics and blue kepreshes. However, they were both baldheaded and modeled painted faces, the mark of royalty. Of course, they were also accompanied by a small detachment of personal guards. As the palanquin made its grand entrance, the kings stood and knelt for their true ruler.

As the slaves lowered their bodies, Piye and Abayomi exited the litter. Abayomi squinted and espied the dry, sandy grounds. Piye placed a hand on Abayomi's shoulder and proceeded into the Bones of Menes.

"Forgive me for my tardiness, my brethren," Piye said with a smile. "The Hour of the Rooster burdens me so."

The kings rose and retook their seats, polished, wooden stools. So did Piye and Abayomi. As soon as they sat, a slave hurried to fan both with a large palm leaf.

Alara spoke first. "It is good to see that you are well, my pharaoh."

"King Alara, I should thank you for your bravery in the recent battle," Piye said in a serious manner. "Send my fondest wish to your sister, Tabiry."

As Alara nodded, Piye switched his attention to King Ottah, the youngest of Kashta. "I pray nightly to Osiris for your father's repose. It was unfortunate you had to lose a father and I a friend in battle."

The twelve-year-old Ottah smiled and nodded. He had a rehearsed response. "He lived only to serve you, my pharaoh."

"With the utmost reverence, my pharaoh, can we get to the matter at hand?" King Bebti said, a bitter old man with little patience. "I have travelled a great distance and in need of rest."

"King Bebti, rest assured, this will not require much of your time," Piye said sarcastically. "This is my son, Abayomi."

All the kings nodded, silently. Abayomi reciprocated with an awkward nod. Piye gave him a reassuring wink before standing as though beginning a dramatic performance. 185

"I will not leave him with chaos!" Piye pleaded. "The Assyrians are a serious threat. The small skirmish we engaged in is but a foresight of Sargon's ambition. It is time for war. Let us not wait for the invasion he will surely invoke. Let us be the sharp tip of the blade. I am demanding we take the battle to him. We must invade Assyria."

"Go to war?" King Ur Atim said as the prudish king folded his legs. "Why should we disturb a cobra's nest?"

King Sadiki coughed profusely. "It is a river that flows into nowhere." The middle-aged Kushite had a long, gray beard and many looped earrings in every facial orifice. "Wisdom is not an inheritance guaranteed by the gods, it seems. I watched Shabaka plummet into that same trap."

"My father was a man of great courage, but he was a man of misguided conviction," Piye said as he sat. "Sadiki, I agreed to marry Khensa to strengthen our bond for times as these. Am I to believe your granddaughter's sacrifice is of little consequence? My kings, it has been prophesied by the gods. I am to lead Egypt through all threats so that my son will receive a land free of war and tyranny. I shall fulfill this request with force, if necessary. I am requesting that each of you summon your finest warriors."

"We appreciate your candor, my pharaoh," King Bebti said with a smirk. "You have the support of Khmun."

"You have the support of Cairo," King Alara said expediently.

"Khartoum will support our pharaoh," King Ur Atim said with hands clasped.

King Sadiki nodded while coughing. "Abu Simbel will honor our pharaoh."

King Ottah's vassal whispered in the young king's ear before he responded with eagerness. "You have the support of Thebes, my pharaoh."

Piye smiled and extended a hand to the sky. "We have concluded! Let us drink in harmony. I have acquired a rare wine from the coast of the Adriatic."

Suddenly, multiple servants entered the space with carafes. The women were scantily clad in silk tunics. The kings were provided goblets, and the servants began filling them. There was congeniality in the air. Piye gazed at the men and smiled with contentment.

"Your wine, my pharaoh," a soft voice came from over Piye's shoulder.

As Piye reached for the goblet behind him, he looked up to his grandest astonishment. He saw the face of a female Kushite. He stumbled from his stool in horror. The woman was Mosi.

"Father!" Abayomi reached for Piye.

Piye's stare fishtailed as he breathed heavily. He saw the look of concern from the kings. Several servants rushed to help the pharaoh to his feet. Mosi was no longer present. The servant girl had an opal face he had never seen. She looked devastated.

"Father, are you okay?" Abayomi cried.

"Yes," Piye said as he brushed himself off. "Be of no concern everyone. I simply mishandled this rickety stool. It is fine, girl. Hand me my wine."

"It appears the wine might be stronger than what it appears," King Sadiki whispered to his vassal with a humorous tone.

^^^

The construction of the queen mother's pyramid was near completion. Ten thousand slaves from throughout the dynasty saw to its construction. The limestone blocks came from as far away as Lower Egypt. The main pyramid stood as tall as five hundred feet and was coated in liquified bronze. It housed the burial chamber, the queen mother's gateway to Duat. Also, it held the shrine to Seth, reachable through the rune- adorned vestibule. The satellite pyramid was home to her prized flora and relics from childhood. The stone walls in cardinal directions were nearly complete.

Bahiti and Gahiji beheld the construction from the towering comforts of the veranda of her personal chamber within the Pyramid of Great Gatherings. Gahiji gaped at Bahiti as the Great Royal Wife espied the brutal servitude with a moment of despondency. The sounds of forced labor was in earshot since the pyramid was located within Napata's walls.

"She wished to enter with my father," Bahiti said softly. "Piye forbade it. He can be cruel. How can we share the same seed?"

"The gods rarely explain themselves," Gahiji replied.

"What we do in this life means nothing."

Bahiti smiled for a few seconds. "No, I suppose they do not."

Gahiji held her hands. "War is upon us. Let us flee this chaos. We could leave together on a ship, and sail to a place no one would find us."

Bahiti caressed his right cheek. Her index finger slid down the long cobra tattoo. "Perhaps, in time. I have unfinished duties to complete."

Gahiji pulled her closer, ignoring all possible witnesses to their infidelity. "Ever since she died, I thought about you and what could have been. I have carried that anger for far too long."

"You must carry it a bit longer," Bahiti said sternly.

"Bahiti, do not test my resolve!" Gahiji said as he pushed her away.

She kissed him, long and passionately. Gahiji embraced her small frame. Her bosom pressed against his leather tunic. He removed her tunic's top and consumed the nape of her neck. She, in turn, removed his breastplate and started pecking his muscular, battle-scarred chest.

Dusk fell upon Napata, and the cawing of spur-winged geese permeated the night sky.

^^^

The next morning, Catena was packing her rarities with 189

two other Sicilian women. They were tasked to have every-thing packed for the trek north, upon which they would take a merchant vessel to Messana. Catena and Fadil planned to reunite after he convinced Piye to allow their courtship.

"This all need to be packed by nightfall," Catena said to the women in Sicilian.

As they loaded the small crates onto the horse-drawn wagon, a small Egyptian boy in a ragged tunic approached the ladies. He handed Catena a piece of parchment. "The chief advisor sent me to give you this."

Before Catena could provide him with gratuity, the lad scampered away. Catena chuckled and read the message.

Meet me at the garden at the Hour of the Hyena. I have a parting gift. Fadil

Excitement overcame her. She crumpled the message and stuffed it in her bosom. She wiped the grime of relo-cating from her face and stroked her long, dark hair. Fadil had promised to pursue her father's release from Sargon's clutches. Her past was filled with turmoil and struggle, yet Catena had discovered love. It wasn't the heart bleeding kind. It was a feeling of belonging and admiration. Fadil ignored his newfound knowledge of her life of espionage and deception. He wanted her by his side when he took his place as ruler of Egypt.

Later that evening, Catena went to the zoological gar-den. She wore the A-line cotton skirt and onionskin shawl that she had worn earlier in their courtship. As she ap-proached the gated, private zoo, she was met by two of

Fadil's guards with long spears.

"I am to meet the chief advisor inside," Catena said flatly.

The guards looked at one another in bewilderment. They had learned that their commander was healing in his private chambers. However, one of the guards had remembered seeing Fadil with the foreigner several moons ago.

"I will escort you to the chief advisor," the large man said.

"Such kindness is not necessary," Catena said as she passed both men and entered the garden.

Catena walked several hundred feet and scanned the grounds in search of Fadil. The illumination provided by the string of torches was inadequate at best. She smiled as she passed the bonobo ape, a beast more curious about her presence than angered. After making pseudo sign language with the ape. She moved on to the Katanga lion, which was hidden in its den apparently.

Catena stooped down to espy the cage. She tilted her head and made sounds like a cat's meow. Catena wanted to view the tranquil carnivore before departing. She peeked over her shoulder for any other inhabitants. Alas, the place was desolate. Even the caretakers were away doing whatever it is they do in their leisure. Although she was disappointed with not seeing the lion, her heart was still beating heavily with anticipation of seeing Fadil soon.

Catena's hand fondled the bars of the cage until she noticed something peculiar. The heavy padlock was missing, 191 and the door to the cage was unlocked. There was only a metal latch separating her and the lion. Startled, Catena stood and backpedaled, unaware of the shadowy figure standing behind her. It was the sinister man who visited her at her chambers. The cloaked, pale man had the piercing eyes of a wolf and the physical attributes of a leper. He grabbed her from behind and tightened his arm around her neck, shutting off a healthy flow of oxygen.

"Sargon is very unhappy," he whispered through his gritted teeth.

"It was a foolish errand. His brother despises him beyond reproach," Catena gasped. "In time, I can convince him to take his rightful place as pharaoh."

"Alas, it is too late," he said with a smile as he put a dagger to her throat. "The pharaoh has already declared war with our master. Please, do not feel that this is something I enjoy doing."

"So, this is my fate? You will kill me among the beasts?" she pleaded.

"Too messy," the man said before unlatching the cage gate and thrusting Catena into the cage. He lowered the latch and inserted the missing padlock.

Catena lifted herself from the dirt floor and panted. Her assailant then banged on the bars with his dagger. The sound of a growl alerted Catena as the lion slowly made its way from the den. When she turned back to the bars, the man was gone. She was horrified as the giant cat moved in her direction. Tears streamed down her cheeks, and she began whispering prayers to Demeter. The lion paused for a moment before pouncing. As her blood blended with ground, Catena was dragged back to the heavy brush that was the lion's den. As her heart stopped beating, the lion consumed her innards. Her sight began to fade. She remembered her childhood and the days of frolicking on the hills on the Messana coast.

Chapter Twenty-Four

Piye and Abayomi knelt before the stone slab altar at the Temple of Osiris. The spacious building was empty of priests. Only Piye's personal guards were posted outside the temple of prayer. Father and son were dressed in ceremonial garb, which consisted of white, cotton robes over satin tunics. Two months had passed since the queen mother's death.

"You are the son of a pharaoh, Abayomi," Piye said as he gazed at the statue of Osiris. "One day, you will reign."

Abayomi stared up at his father. "I fear I will fail you, father."

Piye looked down at Abayomi. "Nonsense. You are my son, alive and healthy. You have given me more than you have ever imagined. You will not ever fail me."

"I failed my mother," Abayomi said as he sulked.

"Every son fails his mother to some respect."

"Did my brother?" Abayomi said.

"In time, we will discuss Theoris. Let us pray."

They each clasped their hands and bowed before the altar. Together, they chanted The Cannibal Hymn to Pharaoh Unis, the ancient text handed down by kings for over a thousand years. The dimly lit chamber relied on torchlight to illuminate the darkness from outside.

"The sky rains down. The stars darken. The celestial vaults stagger. The bones of Aker tremble. The decans are stilled against them, at seeing Pharaoh rise as a Ba. A god who lives on his fathers and feeds on his mothers.

"Pharaoh is Lord of Wisdom, whose mother knows not his name. Pharaoh's glory is in the sky, his might is in the horizon. Like his father, Atum, his begetter.

"Though his son, Pharaoh is mightier than he.

"Pharaoh's Kas is behind him. His guardian forces are under his feet. His gods are over him. His Uraeus-serpents are on his brow. Pharaoh's guiding-serpent is on his forehead: she who sees the Ba good for burning. Pharaoh's neck is on his trunk.

"Pharaoh is the Bull of the Sky, who shatters at will, who lives on the being of every god, who eats their entrails, even of those who come with their bodies full of magic from the Island of Flame.

"Pharaoh is one equipped, who assembles his Akhs. Pharaoh appears as this Great One, Lord of those with hands. He sits with his back to Geb, for it is Pharaoh who weighs what he says, together with Him, whose name is hidden, on this day of slaying the oldest ones.

"Pharaoh is Lord of Offerings, who knots the cord, and who himself prepares his meal. Pharaoh is he who eats men and lives on gods, Lord of Porters, who dispatches written messages.

"It is Grasper-of-the-top-knot who is Kehau, who lassoes them for Pharaoh. It is Serpent Raised head who guards them for him and restrains them for him. It is He-upon-the-willows who binds them for him. It is Courser, slayer of Lords, who will cut their throats for Pharaoh, and will extract for him what is in their bodies, for he is the messenger whom Pharaoh sends to restrain. It is Shezmu who will cut them up for Pharaoh, and cooks meals of them in his dinner-pots.

"It is Pharaoh who eats their magic and gulps down their Akhs. Their big ones are for his morning meal, their middle-sized ones are for his evening meal, their little ones are for his night meal, their old men and their old women are for his incense-burning. It is the Great Ones in the North of the sky who light the fire for him to the cauldrons containing them, with the thighs of their eldest. Those who are in the sky serve Pharaoh, And the butcher's blocks are wiped over for him, with the feet of their women.

"He has revolved around the whole of the two skies. He has circled the two banks. For Pharaoh is the great power that overpowers the powers. Pharaoh is a sacred image, the most sacred image of the sacred images of the Great One. Whom he finds in his way, him he devours bit by bit.

"Pharaoh's place is at the head of all the noble ones who are in the horizon. For Pharaoh is a god, older than the oldest. Thousands revolve around him; hundreds offer to him. There is given to him a warrant as a great power by Orion, the father of the gods.

"Pharaoh has risen again in the sky. He is crowned as Lord of the Horizon. He has smashed the backbones and has seized the hearts of the gods. He has eaten the Red

Crown. He has swallowed the Green One. Pharaoh feeds on the lungs of the wise. And likes to live on hearts and their magic.

"Pharaoh abhors against licking the coils of the Red Crown. But delights to have their magic in his belly. Pharaoh's dignities will not be taken away from him.

For he has swallowed the knowledge of every god. Pharaoh's lifetime is eternal repetition. His limit is ever-lastingness. In this his dignity of: If-he-likes-he-does. If-he-dislikes-he-does-not. He who is at the limits of the horizon, for ever and ever.

"Lo, their Ba is in Pharaoh's belly. Their Akhs are in Pharaoh's possession, as the surplus of his meal out of the gods. Which is cooked for Pharaoh from their bones. Lo, their Ba is in Pharaoh's possession. Their shadows are removed from their owners, while Pharaoh is this one who ever rises and lasting lasts. The doers of ill deeds have no power to destroy, the chosen seat of Pharaoh, among the living in this land. Forever and ever."

Piye faced Abayomi. "A pharaoh must always put the land before the people closest to you. Remember what I have said."

Abayomi nodded, having accepted his newfound destiny and indoctrination. He grew to adore Piye. Thoughts of his mother soon dissipated. Like most followers of the strong pharaoh, the boy succumbed to Piye's ability to sway his most contemptuous critics.

^^^

Bahiti visited Fadil at his bedside as he recovered from his reaggravated shoulder and leg wounds. He was given opium poppy to numb the pain and restricted to his private quarters. He was under constant guard in case Gahiji wished to finish the skirmish. Handmaidens tended to his needs and were replacing his bandage when Bahiti appeared with her ladies-in-waiting. Sunbeams streamed into the chamber and gave the lotus flowers a majestic appearance. The pond was stagnant and glimmered under the rays.

"He killed mother. I know it," Fadil said as he coughed.

Bahiti pretended to ignore his comment. "You must focus on getting better, Fadil. Our family must remain intact for the coming wars."

Fadil grunted as he sat up on his bedding. His handmaidens worked around his sudden movement. He peeked at his wounded thigh before it was rebandaged.

"When I am well, he will feel my blade," Fadil said. "Gahiji will not be as fortuitous as last time. I think his dagger was laced with toad poison."

Bahiti raised her hand. "Leave us!" The servants exited accordingly.

"The next time he will kill you, Fadil," Bahiti said with a disapproving tone.

"So be it. I am not a coward. Bahiti, our mother is dead, and we are to do nothing?"

"When nothing seems to be nothing, something can rise

easily from nothing," Bahiti said as she placed a sympathetic hand on his forearm.

"Imprudent words of a woman," Fadil said with a wince.

Bahiti gave him a sympathetic stare. "Get better, brother."

Fadil watched as his sister appeared to float away in her long gown. It was cold especially that day. Winter had pervaded Napata, and bitterness ran rampant throughout the empire.

^^^

Piye returned to the courtyard for another ride on Kawa. It was chilly morning, and frost had settled on the desert floor. Piye wore his usual riding garb with the edition of a heavy, wool cloak for protection from the elements. On horseback, Piye negotiated several obstacles. Kawa hurdled each one effortlessly. The highest hurdle remained; a four-foot jump Kawa made easily in the past.

As Kawa neighed with nostrils aquiver and pulsating with steam, Piye saw a manifestation of Mosi from the corner of his eye. The ghostly figure was gone when he turned that direction. The pharaoh breathed deeply and pulled sharply on the reins. He laughed boisterously. He attributed his visions to fatigue, which seemed appropriate since his mind was occupied by the Assyrians.

Kawa danced around before Piye gained control. He kicked his heels into the stallion's underbelly and screamed a battle cry of old. In an instant, Kawa galloped rapidly towards the hurdle fifty feet away. As steam streamed from both their orifices, Piye thought of the glory he would receive once he disposed of Sargon. He marveled at the empire he would leave Abayomi and the deference he would command from the people.

Piye braced for the final jump, and he felt uninhibited at that moment. Kawa glided through the air until the unthinkable occurred. The horse did not clear the pole and fell victim to uncontrolled gravity. Piye was thrown from his saddle and plummeted to the hard sands. His back snapped on impact. However, that was the least of his problems. The unbalanced steed fell atop Piye, crushing his chest cavity. Kawa screamed as he floundered with two broken legs. There were no witnesses.

So, the pharaoh took his final breaths beneath his favorite joy. As blood gushed from his nostrils, mouth, and ears, Piye was stunned by his failure to negotiate a trick he had done almost daily. He spoke incoherently for several seconds before he managed a single word.

"Theoris."

Then there was darkness.

^^^

A stable boy discovered Piye two hours later, and soon, the courtyard was filled with the pharaoh's personal guards and Gahiji. Musims guarded the exits to disallow anyone from entering or exiting the open field. Piye and Kawa had been removed in preparation for royal mummification and burial. Gahiji inspected the scene and examined the heavy obstacle responsible for the misfortune. He reconstructed the heavy hurdle's splintered remains. Gahiji noticed that the wooden structure had been freshly painted, and the wood was cut recently. Using his khopesh as a guide, he measured the uprights. They were about six feet in length, quite a feat for any breed of horse. *Why would Piye attempt such an act?*

An officer in the personal guard approached the chief commander. "The men have searched the grounds thoroughly, Chief. We will discover if there is any treachery."

Gahiji tossed an upright aside. "Cease the investigation. There has been no mischief. The pharaoh succumbed to misfortune."

^^^

Nearly a month had passed since Piye's grand funeral. Thousands surrounded the pyramid constructed in his honor. It was erected on the outskirts of Napata and was encased in golden limestone. At its apex sat a brazier that burned continuously. The flames could be scene from as far as Kerma.

The pharaoh was buried alongside his mother, Kawa, and his other prized horses, which were immediately executed to accompany their master to the afterlife. The priests of every sect were freed, and they oversaw the ritualistic event. Bahiti and Fadil mourned Piye and the queen mother by evoking the Law of Redemption, which called for prayer in Napata's center nightly from the people.

Thus, it was time to name a new pharaoh. Abayomi was renamed Tantamani and given the title pharaoh by the high priests. However, Fadil was appointed pharaoh regent until the young pharaoh came of age. Fadil was called Taharqa from that day forward. Bahiti was removed as the Great Royal Wife and served the rest of her days as a high priestess of Osiris.

The day Abayomi was proclaimed pharaoh had arrived. Piye's former chamber was now his. He and Fadil sat alone. They held hands as the roar of outside cheer had risen within earshot. Dressed in gold-hued, leather tunics that reached their knees and wigs of wool, they both wore a kepresh, also known as the Blue Crow.

"Do not be afraid," Fadil said with a smile.

Abayomi nodded and allowed himself a moment of respite in his memories.

"The bath was a good idea, Chenzira," Abayomi said with his eyes closed. He looped his fingers through the pleasant steam bath.

"It is," Chenzira replied. "We are missing fruit to help us embrace this moment. I have not had a warm bath since…" Chenzira searched his thoughts for a couple seconds. "I have not bathed properly since I got away."

"Where did you escape from, from whom?" Abayomi was intrigued. He did not truly know much about Chenzira's past. He only knew that the young man was distant at times.

Chenzira was silent. He stared at Abayomi in awe of his innocence and in resentment of his naivety. He could not bring himself to recall those days. Pain became his closest friend, and perseverance was a nearby illusion that came to his rescue.

"Do you trust her, Abayomi?"

"Yes," Abayomi said without hesitation.

"I guess it is time to part ways. I'll find one of the ladies to give us the fruit we need," Chenzira said as his wiry frame exited the pool.

Abayomi shook his head as Chenzira darted away. He practiced holding his breath under water, the way Chenzira taught him. He came above water seconds later, coughing and choking. He didn't have to relieve himself.

Abayomi returned to the present with a smile. They stood and Fadil guided the boy to the veranda. Below, there were ten thousand or more gathered to celebrate their new pharaoh. Abayomi raised a single hand as the crowd's cheer grew louder. Fadil's eyes met Gahiji's miraculously, and the pharaoh regent gave him a look of conviction. Gahiji bowed and disappeared into the crowd. Fadil and Abayomi shared an amiable stare as the mass chanted.

"Glorious is the soul of Re!"

"Glorious is the soul of Re!"

Epilogue

Sargon released the string of the bow, and the arrow hit the bullseye of the target. Splinters flew as the missile went through and through. The children behind him clapped at his success. The courtyard of his illustrious, walled palace was his home from which he ruled. The stone structure featured a moat and a bridge with guards patrolling, dutifully. On that morning, he spent it showcasing his archery skills to his son and nephews.

Sargon the Second was a handsome middle-aged man. His body was toned, and he stood nearly six feet. His long beard and black hair gave him a younger appearance. The elaborate robe he wore signified his royal standing and fine upbringing. A charismatic man, Sargon had a serene disposition that hid the fire that blazed in his heart.

The game was interrupted by a young Assyrian vassal in a silk, embroidered robe. The man handed Sargon a scroll. "This just arrived, my lord."

Sargon read the parchment with a smile. "It seems Piye is no longer among us. When I offered my hand in friendship, he chose to spit in it."

"We have lost contact with his brother," the vassal said as he bowed. "How shall we proceed, my lord?"

Sargon returned the scroll. "Now, they will accept my fist as my enemy. Have the council convene in my throne room in the next hour."

As the vassal departed, Sargon gazed at the boys next to him, Sennacherib, Ashurbanipal, and Shamash-shuma-ukin. He handed the longbow to his son, Sennacherib. The enthusiastic adolescent grabbed the bow and loaded an arrow. He aimed at the wooden target some forty feet away.

"Careful, you must breathe deeply," Sargon whispered. "Your opponent will often be unpredictable. Release when your eyes command you."

The boy let the arrow fly, and it landed just below his father's. Sargon smiled and nodded at the pleased youth. His nephews began jostling for their turn to try.

"Fate is already written," Sargon said to himself. "They will know how unforgiving fate can be."

About Author

R L Scott was born and raised in Cleveland, Ohio and now resides on the west coast of the US.

Other Works

The Lion's Brood: The Story of Hannibal / ISBN: 978-1-7363861-0-1

Beyond Mali / ISBN: 978-1-7363861-1-8